ANIMORPHS®

<MEGAMORPHS #4>

Back to Before

K.A. Applegate

AN
APPLE
PAPERBACK

SCHOLASTIC INC.
New York Toronto London Auckland Sydney
Mexico City New Delhi Hong Kong

Art direction and design by Karen Hudson/Ursula Albano
Cover illustration by David B. Mattingly

ISBN 0-439-17307-8

12 11 10 9 8 7 6 5 4 3 2 1 0 1 2 3 4 5/0

Printed in the U.S.A. 40

First Scholastic printing, May 2000

For Michael and Jake

Back to Before

CHAPTER 1
Jake

"Help me."

I tried to get up. There was a body lying on me. Hork-Bajir. His wrist blade was jammed against my side.

I tried to lift up with all four legs, lift the dead thing off me. But I only had three legs. My left hind leg lay across the bright-lit floor, a curiosity, a macabre relic. Tiger's paw.

I tried to slide. That was better. The floor was wood, highly polished. Slick with blood, animal, alien, human. I reached out with my two front paws, extended the claws, and dug them into the wood. They didn't catch at first. But then my right paw chewed wood and I gained traction.

A voice said, "Help. Please help me."

I dragged myself slowly, carefully, gingerly out from beneath the bladed alien. The pain in the missing leg was intense. Don't let anyone ever tell you animals don't feel pain. I've been a lot of animals. Mostly they feel pain.

<Jake? Jake?>

It was Cassie. <Yeah. I'm here.>

With a lurch I was free of the weight pressing me down. I rose, shaky on three legs. Looked around through the tiger's eyes.

It was a fabric-cutting room. A design house. You know, dresses no one actually wears. The kind of stuff you see on *Style With Elsa Klensch* as you're flipping channels.

Fashion? Strange front organization for the Yeerks. Why?

There were hugely wide, long tables covered in cloth. One tilted up weirdly, one leg had been broken off entirely. Kind of like me. There were big rolls of patterned fabrics on that end that weighed the table down and made it balance, like a seesaw, not up, not down.

Overhead there were banks of brilliant fluorescent lights. Splashes of stylish neon on the bare brick walls. Bodies everywhere. Blood. Slashes of it.

<Cassie?>

I saw the wolf limp out from behind an overturned cart. She was alive.

I felt a wave of relief. The last I'd seen of Cassie she was in trouble.

In the distance, out through the big doors, down the dark hallway, I heard the hoarse vocals of a grizzly bear. Rachel. Not fighting, not anymore, just raging, raging. Roaring with the frustration of a mad beast looking for fresh victims and finding none.

Marco was already demorphed. A kid. My age, but he looked so young to me. My best friend. He'd demorphed to human because the alternative was bleeding to death from the gash across his gorilla throat.

Demorph to human. All better. No pain.

"I'm cold. I'm cold, help me," the voice called.

<Make sure he can't see you,> I warned Marco.

Rachel came lumbering back into the room, eight hundred pounds of shaggy brown fur and railroad spike claws and a vaguely quizzical grin that hid sharp canines. <Where's Tobias?>

I didn't answer. I didn't know the answer.

Rachel began shoving and lifting Hork-Bajir bodies. She found Tobias, a crumpled hawk. He was breathing.

<Tobias, morph!>

I heard the clop, clop of delicate hooves. Ax was behind me. As alien as any of the dead lying around us. A dainty centaur. The body of a blue deer or antelope, with an upper body not so different from humans. A head that was very different, mouthless, with two extra eyes perched atop movable stalks. His long, dangerous tail was wet with gore.

We'd been in many fights. This one was bad. This one would invade my sleep and wake me sweating and crying.

<Tobias! Listen to me! Go to human!>

"Someone . . . so cold . . . help . . ."

Cassie trotted over to Rachel. She demorphed swiftly.

So good to see her. Healthy. Whole. Beautiful in my eyes.

"He's okay," Cassie assured Rachel. "I think he's just stunned."

As if to prove her right Tobias ruffled a wing and said, <Hey! What? Oh. Oh. I'm alive.>

<More or less,> Rachel growled. <That was a crazy thing to do, you idiot! You dive-bomb a Hork-Bajir?>

<You know?> he said. <Thinking back now, it was crazy.>

<Idiot,> Rachel said. But she managed to put an awful lot of affection into that one insult. Tobias had saved her life, nearly ending his own.

I limped over to the one injured human in the room. A human-Controller. An enemy. A man, maybe twenty years old. A human with an alien slug in his head.

"Help me," he said to the tiger's face looming above him. "I'm cold. Help me."

He was cut. Badly. It was a Hork-Bajir slash. Friendly fire, that's what it's called when one of your own troops accidentally injures you. Kills you. Hork-Bajir in the middle of violence slashed one of their comrades.

<Leave him, Yeerk,> I said. <Let him alone, at last. Get out of his head. Let him do this last thing as a free human being.>

His face was pale. White. Waxy, like a white candle. Someone had smashed his head, mangled his ears. I recognized the marks of a tiger's claw. His brown eyes stared up at me.

"I can't get out," the Yeerk inside his head said to me. "The ears are blocked. Can't get out. I'm trapped."

<We have to get out of here,> Ax said. <They may send reinforcements.>

"I'm cold," the human-Controller said. "Just . . . just get me a blanket or . . ."

<Prince Jake,> Ax prodded.

"I'm scared. Does that . . . does that make you happy, Andalite?" the dying man said.

To the Yeerks we were Andalites. The morphing technology is Andalite science, far beyond anything a human was yet capable of. So to them we were Andalites, a misunderstanding we deliberately fostered.

Ax was the only true Andalite in our group.

<No. It doesn't make me happy,> I said.

"The pain . . . can't you help me? Cold. Help me."

<Come on, Jake.> It was Marco. He'd remorphed. To osprey this time. We needed to escape. The air was our surest way out. Grow wings and fly. Fly and put it all behind us. Pretty soon we'd be joking. Laughing. Trying anything that would make us forget what we'd seen.

What we'd done.

"Help . . ."

<Let's go,> I said.

I demorphed. Out of sight of the doomed Controller. Then I grew falcon's wings and flew out through a window Rachel opened with her fist.

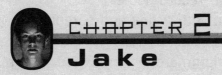

Chapter 2
Jake

My name is Jake.

I live in a normal American city, in a normal American state.

I love my mom and my dad. I even love my big brother, Tom. I like basketball and hate math and get a little down when it rains for more than one day. I think those little Audi TT's are cool but if I had the money, and was old enough, I'd probably drive a Jeep.

I live on burgers and fries and have never voluntarily consumed a brussels sprout.

My room is a mess. My homework is late. My class notes are so disorganized they cannot be read by anyone except Marco, who has been living off my notes for five years or more, and sometimes has to interpret them for me.

I cried the day Michael Jordan retired. And I can still tell you what time it was, what day, week, month, hour, minute, and second, what I was wearing and what I was eating when Mark McGwire banged his record homer.

I'm a kid. A kid with a dog and parents and teachers and friends. Just a kid.

I have these nightmares. Sometimes I'm a termite, trapped inside a piece of wood, can't get out and the clock is ticking, ticktock, ticktock, can't escape, wooden walls and blackness all around me, pressing me tight.

Sometimes I'm falling. Flying and my wings just aren't there and I'm a mile up in the sky, falling, and thinking, *I can't fly! I can't fly!*

Sometimes still, even now, I see the dark red eye of Crayak and feel his malice reaching for me all across the millions of light-years.

But the worst dream is just me and Cassie. And we're standing in the forest somewhere. She's outlined in light. You know, like there's a bright light hidden behind her. And it's almost like she's shining. And there's this cave. And I'm telling her to go in, and she's looking at me with trust in her eyes, looking at me and loving me and believing in me and trusting me and I'm telling her to go into the cave.

I'm the leader of the Animorphs. I don't know how that happened. It was some doom pronounced by Marco. Why me? Because, Marco said. Because it has to be.

We were five kids taking a shortcut home from the mall at night. There was a ship. There was an alien. There was the destructive worm of knowledge: You are not alone. You are not safe. Nothing is what it seems. No one is who they seem to be.

The knowledge of betrayal and terror. The awareness of evil.

And then, the power.

The power made us responsible, see. Without the power the knowledge would have just been a worm of fear eating up our insides.

Bad enough. But it was the power that turned fear into obligation, that laid the weight on our unready shoulders.

We could become any animal we touched, the Andalite told us.

Power enough to win? No. Power enough to fight? Ah, yes. Just enough, little Jake, here is just enough power to imprison you in a cage of duty, to make you fight.

"Help me. I'm cold."

Another battle. Another horror.

Couldn't anything make it end? Was there no way out? Was I trapped, fighting, fighting till one by one my friends died or went nuts?

I lay on my bed. Stared up at the ceiling.

"Help me. Please. I'm cold."

Into the cave, Cassie.

All for what? For nothing. To delay the Yeerks, but never to win. And someday, to lose.

Was there no way out?

"There's always a way out, Jake the Mighty," a voice said. "My lord Crayak holds out his omnipotent hand to you, Jake the Yeerk Killer. Jake the Ellimist's tool."

I sat up. I knew the voice.

The Drode stood by my desk. It wasn't large. It perched forward like one of those small dinosaurs. It had mean, smart eyes in a humanoid head. It was wrinkled, dark green or purple maybe. So dark it was almost black. The mocking mouth was lined with green.

The Drode was Crayak's creature, his emissary, his tool. Crayak was . . . Crayak was evil. A power so vast, so complete that only the Ellimist could keep him in check. A balance of terror: evil and good checking each other, limiting each other, making deals that affected the survival of entire solar systems.

"Go away," I said to the Drode.

"But you called me."

"Go back to Crayak. Leave me alone."

The Drode smiled. He got up and moved

closer. Closer till his face was only inches from my own.

"There *is* a way out," the Drode whispered. "Say the word and it never was, Jake. Say the word, Jake, and you never walked through the construction site. Say the word and you know nothing. No weight on your shoulders. Say the word."

"Go away," I said through gritted teeth.

"How long till your cousin Rachel loses her grip? You know the darkness is growing inside her. How long till Tobias dies, a bird, a *bird*! How can he ever be happy? How long till Marco is forced to destroy his own Controller mother? Will he survive that, do you think? How long, Jake, till you kill Tom? Then what dreams will come, Jake the Yeerk Killer?"

"Get out of here. Crawl back under your rock."

"It will happen, Jake. You know that. The cave. The day will come. You know what the cave is, Jake. You know what it means, that dark cave. You know that death is within. When she dies, when Cassie dies, it will be at your word, Jake."

I covered my face with my hands.

"My master Crayak offers you an escape. In his compassion Great Crayak has struck a deal with that meddling nitwit Ellimist. Crayak would free you, Jake. Crayak would free you all. All will be as it would have been if you had simply taken a different path home."

I saw that moment again. At the mall. Deciding whether to take the safe, well-lit, sensible way home. Or the route that would take us through the construction site, and to a meeting that would change everything.

Undo it. Undo it all. No more war. No more pain and fear and guilt?

"Just one word, Jake," the Drode whispered. "No . . . no, *two,* I think. One must not sacrifice good manners. Two words and it never was. Two words and you know nothing, have no power, no responsibility."

"What words?"

"One is Crayak. The other is *please.*"

I wanted to say no.

I wanted to say no . . .

I wanted . . .

CHAPTER 3
Cassie

DAY ONE

We hooked up at the mall. I was there with Rachel.

Rachel is my best friend. No one knows why, least of all either of us. We could not possibly be more different.

Here are Rachel's priorities in order of importance: shopping and gymnastics.

Me, I'm into animals.

Rachel is every cover girl from every *Mademoiselle* or *Seventeen* you've ever seen. Tall, thin, blond hair and flawless complexion, and approximately four hundred shiny white teeth. To make matters worse, she can't just be written off as another fashion bimbo.

She's not mean. She's not a snob. She is not

a member of any clique. She is her own, one-girl clique. That's the power she has: to be everyone's vision of physical and intellectual perfection and not to care.

Sometimes I wonder where she gets it from. Not the hair, or the clothing, or even her eerie ability to never be messy, dirty, or wet. I wonder where she gets the indifference. I wonder how she can have every boy in school throwing himself in her path, and be indifferent.

Not that she's humble. No. You wouldn't call her humble. She knows she's special. But she's impatient with the whole idea of being popular or whatever.

I get the feeling with Rachel that she's waiting. Impatient. Looking for something more. Moving through life in search of a very different destiny.

Her sports are gymnastics and shopping. She knows she'll never be a great gymnast; she's already about twice as tall as the average gymnast. That part of her interests me but not as much as her shopping.

See, it's not about the stuff with her. It's hunting.

I could never be friends with someone who went out and hunted animals. Sorry, but people who want to shoot deer are not going to be my friends. But when I'm with Rachel at the mall I see the excitement in hunting: the combination of knowledge and instinct and the thrill of stalking and closing in for the kill.

The girl makes the pursuit of a forty-percent-off sweater in just the right size and just the right color seem like a safari to track down a man-eating lion.

"Twenty-five percent off at Express, that's fine," she said. "But, same basic sweater, better mix of fabrics, forty percent off at Structure? Plus, the point is, this sweater goes with the jeans on sale at The Gap *or* the jeans on sale at the department store, and the Express sweater only goes with The Gap jeans."

"I know I'm going to be sorry I asked this," I said, "but how can one sweater that is almost identical to another sweater not go with a pair of basically identical jeans?"

Rachel gave me the look. The look of incredulity and confusion.

"Cassie, you know I love you, but did you just get in from Uzbekistan?" she asked.

"Yes. Yes, Rachel, I just flew in from Uzbekistan."

"Shape. Color. Cut. Waistline." She shook her head in mock pity. "How do you expect to get through life without an appreciation of what goes with what?"

"I expect life will just be one long struggle."

Rachel laughed. No one was more amused by her obsession with shopping than she was.

Like I said, Rachel was waiting for something else. She didn't know what. I sure didn't.

"Don't look," I hissed. "It's Jake."

"I can't look at my cousin?"

"You can look, just don't *look*, that's all I'm saying."

"You mean, don't look at him in a way that will somehow convey to him that you are hot for him? That you want his lips pressed against yours? That you want his big, strong arms wrapped all around you?"

"Yeah, Rachel, that's what I meant. That is exactly what I meant."

Jake is cute. Not cute in a little itsy-bitsy he's-so-cute kind of way. He's a big guy. Not hulking big, just like he's two years older than he really is. He's also smart and funny and modest.

I think he likes me. We sit together on the bus sometimes. Sometimes we seem to accidentally end up near each other at assemblies, or in class.

He's never asked me out. I've never asked him out. Needless to say Rachel finds all this touching, funny, and completely idiotic.

I asked her once, "Do you think he's okay with me being African-American and all?"

She said, "Cassie, I've known Jake all my life.

Believe me, he doesn't know you're black. That's how little he would care. Jake is the one guy out of a thousand who really does care about who you are, not what you look like."

"So, how do I look?" I asked anxiously.

"Like you should be singing eee-yi-eee-yi-oh. You're wearing Wal-Mart overalls with bird poop on the cuffs. You have no makeup on and there's dirt under your fingernails . . . that is just dirt, isn't it?"

I looked down at my fingernails and tried to remember. "Probably dirt. Possibly manure."

"Yeah, well, you compensate for your Old MacDonald clothing sense by being pretty, very smart, very cool, and the most completely real person I've ever met."

"Thanks. Thanks for the last half, anyway."

Jake was with his best friend, Marco. Marco and Jake were not as mismatched as Rachel and I, at least from what I knew. I don't know Marco much at all, just to say "hi" to.

He's small, especially alongside Jake. He has fairly long, dark hair and an olive complexion and a permanently amused expression.

Marco is a comedian. Not a class clown, not a guy who wants to make the teacher mad. He just seems to think the world is funny. I guess a psychologist would call it a defense mechanism. His mom died a couple years ago. Anyway, maybe that's it. Or maybe he's just funny. Anyway, if Jake likes him he must be okay.

Yeah, I don't sound too much like someone with a crush.

There was a third guy with them. This kid named Tobias. He's kind of an unknown to me. He seems like he's kind of latched onto Jake. Jake is too nice to ever tell him to go away, and I could see he was trying to include Tobias in the conversation and all. But Tobias was still standing a little apart. Looking a little uncomfortable, trailing a little behind.

The three of them were coming out of the video game place. Marco looked like he was teasing Jake.

Jake spotted us. For a moment he had a deer-in-the-headlights look. Then he put on his nonchalance.

"Hey, Rachel. Hi, Cassie."

Rachel whispered, "Can I look at him now?"

"You guys going home?" Jake asked. "You shouldn't go through the construction site by yourselves. I mean, being girls and all."

This was a mistake. Jake knew it as soon as the words were out of his mouth, I could see it. But it was too late.

"Are you going to come and protect us, you big, strong m-a-a-a-n?"

Jake started to form a word, but Rachel had him now.

"You think we're helpless just because —"

I cut her off. "I'd appreciate it if they did walk with us. I know you're not afraid of anything, Rachel, but I guess I am."

Rachel shot me a harsh look. I was spoiling her fun.

To get home from the mall we could either go a long way around, which is the safe way, or we could cut through this abandoned construction site and hope there weren't any ax murderers hanging around there.

We took the long way.

Ten minutes of mostly silent walking later, Tobias said, "Hey, what's that?"

I turned and looked in the direction Tobias was pointing. A streak of light, off to our right.

"Meteorite?" Jake suggested.

"Great," Marco muttered. "A meteorite falls out of the sky and totally misses the school. That is so not fair."

We kept walking.

But I had the strangest feeling. Like . . . like going into a room you know, where you're familiar with every stick of furniture, and it's your room, and it's just like it always has been, only somehow, in some way that only appears as a tingling on the back of your neck, it's different.

I shook it off. I had other things to focus on. Like whether Jake was ever going to even hold my hand.

CHAPTER 4
Tobias

DAY SEVEN

I woke up.

Great. Another day.

The couch I was sleeping on was saggy in the middle and smelled of cigarette smoke. But my uncle had gotten drunk and passed out on the floor in my room. So I took the couch.

It was okay, at least that way I could watch TV till I fell asleep.

I was wearing a T-shirt and shorts. I needed to find something to wear. My uncle doesn't do laundry, I do. So I knew exactly what I had available. A nice collection of stuff that could make me look like a complete dork or a complete lowlife, my choice.

My uncle also doesn't buy a lot of stuff for

me. I'm what you'd have to call "low priority" in his life. Half the stuff I had was stuff he'd thrown away. Or else stuff I'd picked up from my aunt's attic whenever I was shuttled off to be with her for a few months.

The food was better at my aunt's. She didn't pass out in my room. She had her own brand of fun. She'd work me like her own personal slave. That's how I knew what was in the attic: I cleaned it out. And she'd keep me out of school to run errands for her or just to "be there" in case she needed me.

At least my uncle let me go to school. He'd have let me go to Australia and not cared. Not a nice feeling knowing that if you were ever kidnapped or whatever, there was no one around to bother and call the cops.

But, hey, that's life. It's worse for lots of kids. Marco's mom died. His dad is a wreck. Marco does everything.

My mom probably died, too. And my dad. I don't know. Everyone just says my mom ran off. Everyone says my dad ran off before I was born. Or sometimes they make up stories, like they both died in an accident. Sometimes I make up stories. The truth, if there ever was any truth, was lost a long time ago.

Doesn't matter.

I put on the least pathetic clothes I could find

and headed for the bus stop. That part was okay. No major hassles at the bus stop, usually. It's not till I'm on the bus that it started. This kid named Andy and his creep sidekick who for some reason was called Tap-Tap, enjoyed kidney punching me. They'd wait till we were getting off the bus, find some way to get up behind me, and when I was all crammed in, they'd nail me once or twice in the back.

I am what they call a bully magnet. I don't know why. I just am.

Used to be these two other guys who had the job of torturing me. Their thing was swirlies. You know, they'd grab me by the ankles and knees and dip my head in the toilet while they flushed.

Used to. This guy named Jake came into the boys' room while they were doing it. He told them to step off. That was it, but he had a way of saying it, I guess.

Those two haven't bugged me since.

I don't think Jake has a big reputation as a tough guy or anything. He's kind of quiet, actually. Almost shy. But there's something about him that makes you take him seriously.

I hung around with him for a while. Totally lame on my part. Jake has a best friend who doesn't like me, I don't think. After a while it was kind of obvious that I wasn't going to be part of that circle of friends.

That was okay. I was still grateful. I guess Jake is who I'd like to be if I could be someone else. But there was a long list of people I'd rather be than me.

I managed to avoid Andy and Tap-Tap on the bus. Which just meant they'd lie in wait for me some other time. Probably it would have just been better to take my beating and move on, without all the suspense of wondering when they were going to get me.

Yeah, right, Tobias. That's a good way to live.

I had to wait all day. Sixth period. I headed for the boys' room. The boys' room is always dangerous for me, but I couldn't hold out all day.

I went in, hoping against hope that a monitor would be in there. But it was me, and two guys I didn't know, and Andy and Tap-Tap.

"Toby, Toby, Toby," Andy called out. "Hey, man, I missed you on the bus this morning. I thought we were friends."

I felt the surge of fear. The ice in my stomach. The urgent desire to wet myself. Tap-Tap moved fast to get behind me, block my escape.

Tap-Tap grabbed me by my shoulders from behind. Should I beg? Would begging do any good?

"Why don't you guys find someone else to pick on," I said. Yeah, that'll work. Whining. Whining will work.

Andy laughed. "But you're so nice and easy," he said. "No one else is as big a wuss as you."

Tap-Tap joined in the laughter. "You're the man, Toby."

Tap-Tap shoved me suddenly forward. Off balance I slammed into Andy.

"Hey! He attacked me, Tap-Tap!"

"Sure did. Toby, man, what's up? Are you getting all violent and stuff?"

"He pushed me," Andy said in mock incredulity.

Wham!

The punch caught me low in my gut.

Wham! Wham!

I was down, twisting my legs around, pretzeling to keep from peeing.

Thunk!

A kick that caught me in the ribs. I rolled over, rolled onto crushed paper towels, head against one of the stall uprights.

Thunk!

A second kick. The pain was shocking. I was scared. They'd really hurt me, this time. Oh, God, they'd really hurt me, who was going to take me to the hospital?

I lay there groaning, back wet from splashed toilet water puddles. I lay there groaning and didn't even realize my tormentors were gone till I saw the faces of the other two guys, the two guys who'd witnessed the whole scene, looking down at me.

"You okay down there?"

I couldn't talk. The pain. The rage. The humiliation choking me.

"Your life doesn't have to be like this," one of them said. "You don't have to be a victim all the time. There's a way out, man."

The other one drew a small card from his back pocket and handed it down to me. "You don't have to be all alone, man. You don't have to be anyone's punching bag."

They walked away. After a while I managed to stand up.

I threw up in the toilet.

I rinsed my face in the sink. I was late for class. Great. That meant a trip to Vice Principal Chapman.

I cried. I was there alone, what did it matter? I cried.

After a while I splashed more water on my face. And then, I looked at the card.

It read THE SHARING.

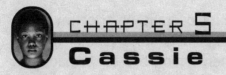

CHAPTER 5
Cassie

I jerked awake.

Eyes wide open.

My covers were a mess. My sheet was twisted around my legs. My pillow was damp with sweat, but the room was cold.

It had happened again. The call. Like a voice, but not a voice. Speaking without words. Images. Pictures, fuzzy, distorted, meaningless.

A wide, grassy field. A glass dome. Trees with pink and blue leaves. And water. Everywhere, water.

It gave me the creeps.

"You have a serious case of the willies," I whispered to myself.

I got up, went to the bathroom, drank some

water, and spent five minutes rearranging my sheets and blankets.

But I couldn't go back to bed. I was wide-awake now. Adrenaline awake.

I could work on some homework. Work on that paper.

No.

I pulled a pair of overalls on over my sleep shirt. Stuck my bare feet into a pair of muddy, unlaced boots. Then I took the boots back off. Boots were not going to make it easy to sneak past my parents' bedroom.

I tiptoed down dark stairs to the living room. The blue display on the VCR was blinking 00:00 again and again. There was a glass on the coffee table. My dad's. I picked it up and carried it to the kitchen and deposited it in the sink.

"That's right, Mom and Dad, I couldn't sleep so I decided to get up at three A.M. and clean house." Yeah, that would work. That wouldn't seem too insane.

Was that it? Was I going crazy?

They say schizophrenia usually appears first during the teen years. I told my mom that once. She said, "Honey, how can anyone tell the difference between a crazy teenager and a regular teenager?"

My dad had laughed, then caught himself.

"Not that we're saying we expect you to be wild or anything, let me make that *perfectly* clear. We're not saying it's okay."

"Okay, Dad. I'll stop my wild and crazy ways."

They laughed. I laughed. We all knew I was not exactly the definition of a wild and crazy girl.

I told the story to Rachel. She said, "Wow, it must be cool to have your parents actually trust you. Man, that would be great if my mom trusted me like that."

"Because then you could get away with anything?"

"Exactly."

I smiled as I was remembering that. I opened the freezer. Hello Ben. Hello Jerry.

No. What if Jake wasn't asking me out because of my thighs?

I staggered, gripped the refrigerator door. It had hit in a wave. The voice. The soundless, wordless voice. Calling from the water.

Oh, man, I really was going nuts.

And it wasn't just the voice. There was this sense of . . . of what? Strangeness? Of things being wrong in some way I couldn't figure out?

Not funny. Not really. What if I was actually mentally ill?

The animals. That was it, I'd go check on the barn.

I went out into the night, out through the kitchen door rather than the front door because my parents were less likely to hear me.

Our barn is the Wildlife Rehabilitation Clinic. Both my folks are vets. My mom works with large animals at The Gardens. My dad handles the clinic, with some help from me.

I guess to a lot of people the barn at night would have seemed eerie. Not to me. There were rows of cages, most full. We had muskrats and raccoons and geese and bats and foxes and deer and a forlorn eagle. All were injured or sick. Many wore bandages. Some were in one form of restraint or another, to keep them from chewing or pecking their own wounds.

They smelled, I guess. Anyway, that's what Marco said when he came —

No, no, he'd never been to the barn. Why would he have ever been to the barn?

"Forget it, Cassie. It's late. It's dark. You're just confused."

My hands shook a little as I funneled a handful of grain into the goose's cage. She didn't need it, really. I just wanted to do something. Something normal.

"How are you feeling? Huh? Yeah, I know, that wing still hurts, doesn't it?"

I went down the row of cages. Tried not to think. Tried not to believe that I was hearing things, imagining things, remembering things that had never happened. The familiarity of the barn soothed me. But within that very familiarity lay a new, unsettling sensation. I saw Jake, pacing. I saw Rachel, restless. Marco lolling on a bale of hay. And up there, up in the rafters, a bird.

A hawk.

I could almost see him. Almost.

Madness. I was losing my mind.

I was losing my mind.

CHAPTER 6

Aximili-Esgarrouth-Isthill

DAY TEN

I raced at full speed, all out, hooves flying, tail tucked down, upper body bowed, stalk eyes straight back to watch the ground that receded from me.

I raced straight for the target, a bundle of sticks tied together to form an extremely crude representation of a Hork-Bajir-Controller.

I ran. Waited. Reveal nothing. No subtle "tells," do not give anything away, he is ready to react to the slightest clue. Would I go left or right? Stop and strike or shoot past and tail whip him?

Fwapp!

I shot past, caught the "head" of the Hork-

Bajir with my blade, and watched it topple onto the ground.

I was panting. Gasping for air. It was my ninth attack. I was tired.

Or maybe it was all in my head. Maybe it was the billions of pounds of pressure, the water that pressed down from all directions.

There was very little hope left within me now. Too much time had passed. If anyone had survived, if my brother Elfangor had survived, he would have found me.

The dome was still intact. It rested on the floor of one of Earth's oceans. It was at a slight angle. I noticed the incline whenever I raced across the vast, open field of grass.

I was not sure how far down I was, how deep. All the instrumentation, the main computers and so on had been in the main section of the ship, spread out along the long corridors, the seemingly endless stalk that connected the dome to the distant engines.

Likewise all small craft. The fighters, the transports, the scout ships. Anything that would fly. All left behind when the dome separated and fell, atmosphere-shrieking and burning, down Earth's gravity well.

Life support was intact. The low-power force field that kept the transparent dome from being crushed by the ocean's pressure, all that was intact. The energy plant would last for a hundred years. The grass would grow, the trees would bloom. The pond had spilled out during a temporary loss of artificial gravity, but it had mostly refilled.

I could live out my life down here. Live out my life in this habitat meant to duplicate life at home.

Except that I could not do that.

Elfangor was probably dead. All the brave warriors with him. We had come out of Zero-space, expecting at most to encounter a few scattered Yeerk ships. But they had been waiting. A full Pool ship with its legion of Bug fighters. And more dangerous still, the sleek black Blade ship of Visser Three.

Our warriors had slaughtered the Yeerks. But we had lost some fighters. And then, the Blade ship had appeared.

Maybe Elfangor had survived, somehow. But if he had, where was he? A fighter's sensors would have located me without great difficulty.

And, unfortunately, the same would be true if the Yeerks were still present in orbit. Sooner or later they would find me. Some Taxxon watching a sensor display would catch the blip of trapped air beneath the waves.

Unacceptable.

I was alone. Without a prince or a partner. A single Andalite *aristh* alone in the submerged dome of a once-great ship. How many light-years from home? What did it matter? I had no ship.

I had called out in bursts of thought-speak. I had used all my energy, all my strength, to fire bursts of thought-speak, seeking Elfangor.

There had been no answer.

No answer for so long.

I let my momentum carry me past the decapitated stick figure, on through the pink-leafed trees. To the dome wall.

It rose up at an angle. I pressed my hand against the plex. Outside, out in the alien ocean, creatures swam by. The variety was startling. I had seen perhaps fifty different species in all, large and small, some apparently harmless and some seemingly dangerous.

Earth.

Elfangor had said little about the place. It was not a major planet. There had been some speculation that its dominant race was on the verge of achieving spaceflight, but aside from a few hundred primitive orbital satellites there had been no evidence.

One thing was sure, the Yeerks in orbit had not been bothered by Earth-based craft.

A long, gray-blue creature swam close by. It scraped the dome, just a short distance from my splayed fingers. It had fins at its sides, a triangular fin that rose from its back, a raked, aerodynamic tail, and eyes that were small, black, and empty. It also had something called a mouth. Many species on the home planet did as well. But this mouth seemed designed as a weapon. There were several rows of jagged triangular teeth.

The fish swam away into the murk. Even when Earth's sun was high in the sky the light down here was dim, rippling, green-blue. During planetary night the dome was so dark that I could stand and watch the faint phosphorescence of passing creatures, like slow comets crossing my personal sky.

Aximili, you have to decide, I told myself.

I could stay in the dome and wait, a week, a month, a year till the Earthers or the Yeerks spotted me.

Or I could venture out of the dome. I had the morphing power. If I could acquire one of these passing creatures I could leave, reach some shore, demorph, and look to make a life among the aliens.

<You have to decide. Stay or go. Wait or leave.>

I did not want to be afraid. But I was, I had to

admit that. The morphing power is only good for two hours at a time. More than that and you are trapped. How far was the shore? How hostile were the inhabitants? Could I hope to survive? The Earthers might be savages. There might be diseases. Predators.

And there was the very real possibility that the Yeerks were already there in force.

You have to decide, I told myself again. *But not yet.*

I headed back toward the target. I stopped still and stared. The head was back in place. Hadn't I . . .

I had. I had seen the head fall. Impossible.

Decide soon, I told myself. *The isolation is having psychological effects.*

CHAPTER 7

Tobias

DAY TWENTY-ONE

"Line up on the cue ball, then draw the line back through your cue, and forward through the ball you're trying to hit, then on to the pocket, right?"

He said "right?" a lot.

"It's all about angles. Pool is geometry. A series of collisions, all at precise angles."

His name was Bill. He was a high-school guy, older than me, obviously. He was my "guide." That's what they call it. When you attend your second meeting of The Sharing they assign you a guide. Someone to answer your questions, someone to hang with you, talk to you.

At first I thought it was some kind of pity

thing. You know, that Tobias kid is such a loser we better put someone with him.

But everyone gets a guide at their second meeting. A guide is a full member of The Sharing. I'm still not sure what that means, a "full member." Bill is a little vague about it.

What he's not vague about is pool. They have two tables in the back of the meeting hall. He has his favorite.

I gripped the cue. Aimed. Tried to see the angles. Tried to see the impacts: cue tip on cue ball, cue ball on seven ball, seven ball on bumper.

"Okay, now relax into it," Bill said. "You want to aim like your life depended on it, then relax like it doesn't really matter, and let your shoulder and arm and hand and eye all work together."

I tried to relax.

Thock!

The cue ball rolled, hit the seven ball that hit the bumper and then curved away from the pocket.

"Sorry," I said.

"What do you mean, sorry? You were off by two percent, maybe. You're getting better. You have an eye for this. You can think in three dimensions. That's good. You wait, when you become a full member you'll be thinking in four dimensions. Five. N-dimensional space."

I had no idea what he was talking about, but I felt my face redden. Pleasure. His compliment may have been sincere or not. I wasn't sure, but I'd take it for what it was worth. There hadn't been all that many compliments in my life.

"Take the next shot," he said. "I want to see how you handle it."

The assumption that I would someday become a full member of The Sharing, that was strange. I'd only attended two meetings. The first time I just kind of wandered around lost, feeling like a dork. I filled out some form with my name and address and social security number and all. The form asked me some personal questions, too. Nothing too personal, but enough to make me uneasy.

But at the same time, even while I was feeling lost, no one made me feel bad. They were kind of welcoming, like me showing up was a cool thing. They didn't press me, didn't try to sell me anything, just kind of let me hang out, watch some kids playing video games, watch other older guys playing basketball out back of the building on a half-court.

When the first meeting was over this guy, this college guy or whatever, came up and shook my hand and asked me personally to come back.

I was back. And now I had Bill teaching me to shoot pool.

I snapped the shot. Cue hit cue ball, hit ball, hit bumper. My ball rolled into the pocket.

"Ah!" I yelled, way too excited.

Bill clapped his hand on my back and gave my shoulder a squeeze. "Cool! Good job, Tobias. That was not an easy shot."

We played pool some more till at last some other guys came up and jokingly demanded the table.

"No problem," Bill said. "My boy Tobias here is getting too good for me already."

It wasn't true. But I *was* better.

"I never played pool before," I said.

"Well, each of us has talents and abilities hidden within us," Bill said. "Who knows what you can do, Tobias? Have you ever had a chance to find out? That's what The Sharing is all about, man. The whole point is we all help each other to become the best people we can become."

I wanted to ask, "Why?" Why would any bunch of people want to get together to help me play pool, or whatever? I mean, what did they get out of it?

But that was just me being cynical. That was me thinking the whole world was like my uncle. It was possible that some people were just nice, right?

There was a chime. A ringing bell, not too loud, but insistent.

Bill groaned. "Time for the 'sit down,'" he said.

"What's a sit down?"

"That's just what I call it. Every couple of meetings or so they have us all get together, talk to us about stuff."

"Like what?"

"You know, like the purpose of The Sharing, and our philosophy and all." He winced. "I shouldn't complain. I mean, The Sharing has totally turned my life around."

"Yeah?"

"Yeah."

"Like how?"

He shrugged and started us toward the main meeting room. "I used to be messed up, man. My folks had a really bad divorce, you know? It was this total mess. Fighting and yelling and lawyers trying to drag me and my sister one way or the other. Sick."

I nodded like I understood.

"Anyway, I got kind of weird up behind all that. Depressed or whatever. Thinking maybe I didn't want to go on living. But The Sharing took me out of all that."

"Yeah?"

He spread his hands wide and smiled. "Not depressed anymore, right? I'm moving on. Dealing with it. Now I have my own plan for the future, you know? Get past all the stuff, get on with my own life, right?"

"Right."

We sat down on folding chairs. There must have been about forty or fifty people there. Kids, older people, white and black and Asian. People in expensive clothes and people more like me. Cool kids, nerds, jocks. All sitting together, talking, like age or race or whatever didn't matter.

I spotted someone I hadn't noticed before. Jake. He was sitting two aisles up, next to his brother Tom.

I was surprised. "That guy up there," I pointed. "Is he a member?"

"Who, Tom? Yeah, Tom is a very senior full member."

I hadn't been talking about Tom, but the information surprised me. "You mean like a senior kid member?"

Bill smiled. "There's no such thing as old or young, not in The Sharing. We don't draw lines like that."

I watched the back of Jake's head as a speaker mounted two steps to a low stage. I watched him as the speaker talked to us about how the lonely individual in society had been overemphasized in our culture. There was no true achievement unless you were part of something greater. You had to serve in order to achieve. You had to join with a larger reality.

"That's why we are called The Sharing," the speaker said. "Together we achieve happiness, fulfillment, meaning. Together, holding each other up, supporting each other, working together to overcome individual weakness, individual failing and pain and hurt."

It sounded good, I guess. I kept watching Jake. I don't know why.

I don't think he knew I was there.

I guess it was pathetic but I thought that if he was a member and I was a member, somehow, someway, stupid thought, lame idea, but somehow I could become him. And not me. Have his life, and not mine.

CHAPTER 8
Marco

DAY TWENTY-FOUR

"You know, you should go out with me," I said.

For a full five seconds Rachel didn't say anything. She just sort of narrowed her eyes and stared straight ahead.

I grinned. She was trapped. Couldn't get away. We were on a field trip to the natural history museum. We'd already looked at the big stuffed elephant. We'd looked at the diorama showing early man cooking barbecue out with the lions. We'd gaped up at the suspended fiberglass whales.

Now we were in the theater where they were about to show us an IMAX film entitled *DNA: Miracle Molecule.* Or some such thing. It was narrated by Paul Shaffer, from Letterman. Weird.

The screen was about the size of an old drive-in theater's screen, but it was so close I could practically reach out and touch it.

So, anyway, we were in the seats next to each other, me and Rachel. Beside her was one of her friends, Melissa Chapman, daughter of the vice principal. The theater was totally full. Rachel was trapped.

"I don't think so," she said at last.

"Is it because I'm roughly three feet shorter than you?"

No answer. Stoic stare.

"Is it that you think I'm cuter than you?"

"Yeah, that would be it."

On-screen Paul Shaffer was saying, "DNA is a *fab*ulous molecule."

An electron microscope slide appeared, showing a DNA molecule as long as a train.

"You know, girls love a guy with a sense of humor."

"Yeah. If he's Leonardo DiCaprio. Adam Sandler, not so much."

Despite myself, I laughed. She could throw it back at me. I liked that.

"Still, we should go out. Do a movie. Eat some burgers. I could make you laugh."

"Actually, I think the mere memory of that suggestion will supply me with plenty of laughter."

She was fast. Sharper than I thought. I'd always assumed she was just this total babe. But she was cool. Funny.

Wow. Fantastic looks and she was funny? How often does that happen?

"You know, I could supply references, Rachel. Plenty of females have enjoyed the company of Marco the Magnificent."

"Females? What species?"

I barked out a laugh and got a loud "shush" from a row back. I guess someone back there really cared what was happening to the five-story green-and-red amoeba pulsating behind Paul's bald head.

I shot a look at Rachel. Was that a faint shadow of a tiny, possibly imaginary smile I saw on her perfect lips? Or was it just a trick of the amoeba light?

I fell silent. Wait. Wait.

"Paul never gets credit for being as funny as he is," she said.

Hah! She was enjoying talking to me. She started it up again. Hah! Well, well, well.

What would Jake say if I started going out with his cousin? He was my best friend. Had been forever. He'd always been there for me. He was the one guy in the world I could absolutely count on.

So if he didn't approve of me and Rachel, hey, it would make me real sad to say "Bye-bye, Jake."

Hah! She liked me. Or at least my sense of humor. No problem-o.

Then . . .

Paul Shaffer's head flickered and melted, erupting in brown goo that merged with what I believe was an invertebrate.

"Awwww, *man*!"

The film had caught and burned. The houselights came up.

"Now we'll never know what happened," I complained. "Did Dave ever make a cameo appearance? Or at least Bif Henderson?"

We all stood up. The kids all managed to control their disappointment. We filed outside, out into the brighter light of the museum proper. I had to struggle to stay up with Rachel. Somehow, and don't ask me to explain it, she had an ability to move easily and quickly through a crowd without ever touching anyone, or being touched in return. Like she was surrounded by a force field.

But I stayed up with her. And by amazingly good luck Melissa made a girls' room run. By herself. Without Rachel. Which is not something you see very often, a pretty girl left vulnerable without some member of her girl gang around to fend off losers.

"So. What do you think?" I asked Rachel. Up close it was hard to ignore the fact that I was looking almost directly up at her. While she was looking at the top of my head.

"I think many things," she said cryptically.

"I mean about . . . abou . . ."

My mouth stopped moving. My throat seized up. I stared. Stared, heart pounding on no oxygen, stared, pushed Rachel aside when she got in the way.

"It's her," I said. I was aware that my voice had cracked. I knew I looked like an idiot. Didn't care. I was far away. I was in some frozen universe watching would could not possibly be.

"Who?" Rachel snapped.

"Mom," I whispered.

"Your mom? So go say hi."

I shook my head slowly, slowly coming out of my paralyzed trance.

She had appeared. Simply appeared. Like materializing out of the air. Like she'd been transported down from the *Star Trek* universe. She was wearing a blond wig, but I wasn't wrong. It was her.

She looked shocked, confused. Lost. Angry. Scared.

Then she was moving away, quickly. Heading for the escalator. Her back was to me.

"My mom! My mom! I have to catch her!"

"Your mom? Isn't she . . ."

"Mom! Mom!" I yelled. I took off. Took off running like an idiot, yelling and running.

CHAPTER 9

Aximili

It took a great deal of patience. Days of patience.

I waited hour after long hour, hope rising and falling, watching the air lock through the transparent bulkhead.

The big creatures would come toward the open air lock, nearer, nearer, but never all the way in.

The air lock was big enough to accommodate four space-suited Andalites. That was its original function, to allow technicians to access the outer surface of the dome.

The only creatures that came into the air lock were smaller finned creatures. These did not seem to possess any natural weapons. Unless, somehow, their fins were far more formidable than they appeared.

In my weeks under the alien ocean I had learned one thing: Earth creatures could be fiercely predatory. The large ate the small.

In this environment there was not much point in being small and weak. I could afford to wait for a chance to acquire something strong. Strong and fast enough, I hoped, to make it safely to the nearest shore, wherever that might be.

So I waited. Waited and invented names for the various creatures who ignored the open cave of the air lock.

Big Mouth. Runny Eyes. Swimming Bird.

And the creature I was after, Blue Blade. This creature seemed to be composed of triangles. Triangular tail, triangular fins, triangular teeth. Its entire body reminded me of a long, flattened triangle. It was blue, the blue-gray of wet steel, not so far different from my own color.

Three days I had waited and waited to spring my trap. Not that I had anything better to do. I exercised. I conjured up absurd scenarios of how Elfangor was alive, had crash-landed among the aliens, and even now was forming an effective guerrilla organization to fight the Yeerks. If anyone could do it, Elfangor could.

But I knew he was dead. Knew it.

<Ah!>

I slapped the panel.

The door materialized. The creature was trapped!

Now what? In order to acquire the creature's DNA I had to physically touch him. He did not look as if he would enjoy being touched. He had to be alive at the moment of acquisition. What if the removal of water killed him instantly?

I instructed the air lock computer to draw off ninety percent of the water. This took a few minutes. When it was done the creature was still able to move, but only in two dimensions. His dorsal fin and part of his back were exposed to the air. His belly scraped the floor.

He kept moving, restless. Afraid? Impossible to say.

<Air lock computer, create a force field to contain the water and prevent its spilling into the outer chamber. Allow me to enter the air lock.>

The computer erected a force field just three feet high, just enough to hold in the water and the creature. Above that three-foot wall of energy was open space. I could easily leap over.

However, leaping back out would be harder. The water would be halfway up my side, submerging my legs.

I waited, watched, timed the creature's movements . . . leaped!

I flew over the invisible wall, splashed into the water. My hooves slipped, I sagged down into the water, the creature whipped toward me, lightning quick.

It surged at me. I stuck out my right hand and pressed its snout. Acquisition usually creates a trance in the acquired creature. Maybe it would work with this creature.

Eventually.

The monster jerked its head, broke contact, swam away, turned in a flash and arced toward me.

Fwapp!

I hit it, flat-bladed, on the snout.

It turned away, but came right back. And now its mouth was open in a grin of triangular teeth.

Fwapp!

I hit it again. And jumped aside a split second before it could bite my front left leg.

<Yah!>

I leaped clear out of the pool and sprawled clumsily on the floor. Water drained off me. Blood, too. Mine. The creature had swiped my haunch with a fin I now realized was quite sharp.

The creature was fast. Aggressive. Not easily discouraged. Perfect for my purpose. Assuming I lived long enough to worry about my purpose.

<Computer, form a force field that will con-

strict the creature into a narrow rectangular space.>

The water receded from both side walls. The creature slammed into the force field, retreated. Tried to turn and suddenly could not.

The Blue Blade was now held within what amounted to a very narrow tank. There was dry floor on either side of him.

<You might have thought of this earlier, Aximili,> I chided myself. I had long since accepted the notion of solipsistic conversation. It was part of a general psychological decay. On at least three occasions I had seen things that were almost certainly not real. Either that or the structure of time itself was different on Earth.

I jumped into the dry space. The creature lay sullen, the vertical gashes behind his mouth worked, open, close, open, close. The one eye on this side glared at me.

I reached and touched the creature's skin. I pulled away surprised. It was rough-textured. I could have abraded the skin from my hand.

I touched him again and focused as we are trained to do when acquiring DNA.

Sharp teeth, sharp fins, speed, aggression, and armored skin — I didn't know how dangerous Earth's oceans might be, but I felt this creature would be safe in them.

CHAPTER 10

Rachel

I don't know why I ran after Marco, but I did.

He was chasing a woman who he couldn't possibly be chasing. Maybe I wanted to help him. But that's not what it felt like. It felt like . . . I don't know, like I liked chasing someone.

That's dumb but it may be the truth.

He raced down the escalator, trying to shove past people. I raced down the steps that paralleled the escalator. I hit the floor first.

"There!" he pointed.

I saw a blond woman fast-walking away through the crowd. A woman pushed a stroller into her path. Marco's ghost shoved the stroller aside and kept moving.

Marco and I pounded after her. No question now, she was running away from us. She was the antelope and we were the wolves.

Of course maybe that's why she was running. Many people would find it disturbing to be chased by a couple of demented teenagers.

In the main foyer she broke into a flat-out run hampered only by the fact that she was punching numbers into her cell phone.

She had maybe a hundred-foot lead. No way some thirty-something mommy was going to out-run me. She ran for the revolving door.

"Hey!"

A man slammed into the glass. She'd knocked him aside.

She was slow getting through the revolving door. *Stupid,* I told myself. *She shouldn't have taken the revolving door. Now we've got her.*

Marco and I reached the revolving door while she was still inside it, just exiting. Marco jumped into the next open section. That's when the woman yanked hard back on the door, spun it backward, caught Marco off balance and nailed him in the face with the brass push-bar.

Marco sat down hard. He grabbed his face. Blood leaked through his interlocked fingers.

"Hey! You okay?" I yelled to him.

"After her! Stay on her!" he yelled and scrambled to his feet.

All right, I told myself. *The boy can focus.*

I went through a side door. There were stone steps, about a dozen, two hundred feet wide, heading down to the busy street.

Business people bustling on the sidewalk below. People coming up and down the steps. Groups. Individuals.

No blond woman.

She couldn't have gotten away. No way. Not enough time. She was here, here in view, one of the three or four dozen bodies in motion.

Wig. It was a wig. The realization came to me in a flash. Marco raced up, stopped, panting beside me.

"She has dark hair," he gasped.

"I guessed that."

He looked back and forth. "I don't see her."

"Has to be here."

"Look for whatever she *wouldn't* be doing," he said. "*Should* be alone, *should* be going down the steps, look for the opposite."

I nodded. Yeah, he was right. He was upset, he was desperate, he thought he was chasing his dead mother, and he still figured that out. Maybe I would go out with him. The little guy had a brain in there.

"There!" I yelled.

She was brunette now, moving with a slow group of old people coming *up* the stairs.

For a split second I met her gaze. Rage. Fury. I hesitated a split second. But a split second later, my own anger answered hers.

You don't scare me, lady.

The wolves were on the scent again. The antelope ran. Onto the sidewalk, shoving, slamming, barreling through businessmen and -women and UPS drivers and hot dog vendors and bike messengers.

We raced along the facade of the museum. She turned a hard right, straight out into traffic.

Give the lady points. She didn't scare easy.

Yellow cabs screeched. Drivers cursed. Fingers were thrust skyward.

She ran, we chased, and we gained.

She ducked into an alleyway. Now we had her. The crowds were her cover. She'd be alone.

I turned the corner first, Marco inches behind me. Dumpsters and overflowing trash cans. A pile of empty bottles all in racks.

She was not in sight. Only two places she could be. Behind the Dumpster. Or behind the stack of bottles.

I looked at Marco. We reached unspoken agreement. He walked softly, sneakers squishing in filth, toward the Dumpster.

"Look out!"

The tower of bottles tipped.

CRASH!

Wham!

Something hit the side of my face. Hard. My eyes rolled in different directions. Tears blurred my vision. A dark shape, moving fast right for me. A bottle in her hand.

Swing!

I ducked, kicked instinctively, and caught yielding flesh. My vision was clearing but I was still wobbly.

She was down on her butt.

She slammed the bottle down on the ground. It shattered, leaving her holding a broken bottle, all jagged, ripping edges.

A deadly weapon.

I backed up, heard Marco yell, "Get your hands off me!"

Someone had him. A man. A large man.

This was going very bad very quickly.

I spun, a nice pirouette. Much easier on the ground than on the balance beam.

I snatched up a bottle and nailed the elbow of the man holding Marco.

"Ah!"

Marco slipped free.

"RUN!" I yelled and yanked him with me.

We ran. Back toward the street. But suddenly two new figures loomed in our path.

The cell phone. The woman had called

for help. Even then some part of my scared, adrenaline-saturated brain wondered what kind of woman could make a call and have tough guys showing up within seconds.

"Back!"

We turned. Trapped. Two big guys behind us. One guy with a sore elbow and Marco's mother ahead of us.

Think fast, Rachel. I slid the toe of my shoe under one of the bottles and flipped it up at the woman. She flinched and we shoved past her.

Great. Now all four of them were behind us. And I didn't see any way out of the alley.

Straight ahead a blank wall. The alley turned right. We turned right, scrabbling and panting and now very seriously scared.

Dead end!

Walls. Walls. Walls.

I tried a door. Locked. Marco tried another. Locked.

Overhead, a fire escape, the kind that lowers on springs when a person is descending. It was drawn up, hanging in midair. Seven feet up?

The three men turned the corner. The woman was gone. I had a feeling it didn't matter. The men looked very serious. Determined.

I stopped short of the tantalizing fire escape. "Marco! Stand right there!" I pointed at a spot on the ground, ten feet away from the fire escape.

I raced over to stand beneath the black-painted wrought iron. Turned, cupped my hands together below my waist.

"Are you crazy?" Marco demanded.

"You have a better idea?"

"Ahhhhhh!" Marco yelled and ran straight at me. Jumped, seated his foot in my cupped hands. I heaved up, timing the movement to use his momentum.

Up he went. Not far. Just enough. He grabbed the bottom of the fire escape, drew it down with his weight. The thing screeched with the strain of rusted metal on rusted metal.

I caught it before it hit the ground and we blew up the stairs, crowding each other, frantic. The springs lifted up the stairs after us out of reach of our pursuers, but we weren't going to stop and toss off any clever comic book, "Take that, villain!" lines.

We were going to climb till we ran out of stairs.

Three stories.

BLAM! BLAM!

At first I couldn't figure it out. What was that incredibly loud noise?

BLAM! BLAM!

"They're shooting at us!" I yelled in outrage.

"Yeah. RUN!"

We topped the fire escape and tumbled over the parapet onto the roof just as something really disturbing happened.

The men stopped firing guns.

They started firing lasers.

CHAPTER 11

Aximili

I stood in the empty air lock. The Blue Blade was long gone. It was time for me to be long gone, too. I considered waiting. But I was waiting for nothing, and I knew it.

More waiting would just be cowardice. No one was coming to rescue me.

I was frightened. There is nothing wrong with admitting that. A warrior who is not afraid when he goes toward danger is a fool. Fear is the reflex that keeps us alive.

I focused on the image of the Blue Blade. Tried to see it in every detail. It was not difficult. I had spent quite a while observing it.

I focused and I began to change.

My four legs dwindled swiftly. They melted up into my body. The floor rushed up toward me.

Suddenly my stalk eyes went dark. I could only see directly ahead of me.

<No!>

I reversed morph. Demorphed. A momentary panic, that was all. I had felt suddenly blind. The three-dimensional world had gone flat.

Stupid. I was annoyed with myself. Obviously the creature I was to morph had only two eyes. I should have been prepared.

I took a last look around. Through the transparent wall into the dome, at the familiar trees, at the grass that had nurtured me. I might never return. I might never again stand on any part of Andalite soil.

No point in being sentimental, I told myself. *You are a warrior now.*

Unprepared, yes. Without a prince or a mission. Too bad. That was how it was. I was alone on an alien world that might be infested with Yeerks. And would, most likely, offer me no viable means of returning to my home world.

A movement. Something out past the door, past the shell of the dome in the ocean itself. It was distorted by the lenses of water and plex.

Distorted, warping in the filtered green sunlight.

Bug fighter!

The shock knocked the wind out of me. Bug fighter! Yeerks! They had found me. They were here. Coming. Yeerks!

I fought the instinct to run back into the dome. NO. That is where they would kill me. Without shields up, with nothing but a weak force field it would be child's play to blow holes through the dome and drown the trees, the grass, and anything else that required air.

Morph. Morph. It was the only way. And quickly.

My ears flattened against my skull and melted away. My arms slid down the length of my torso, hands flattening, stiffening, sharpening, till they formed matched fins.

Following my orders the computer was filling the air lock with water. Cold.

Hurry!

I was almost on my belly. My four hooves remained, absurd remnants. Then, they, too, disappeared and I was a growing, elongating cylinder.

My upper body tilted down, coming into line with the cylinder. My tail blade split in two, forming an upper and lower triangle.

My nostrils drifted across the fluid surface of my face, seemed to crawl across liquefied flesh to stop just behind my stalk eyes, which had, themselves, slid down to opposite sides of my head.

I heard the sickening slurp and slush of internal organs reforming, relocating, disappearing altogether, being replaced by more primitive structures.

My fur that had been melting wax now hardened and congealed, forming the stiff, abrasive skin of the Blue Blade.

Faster! Hurry! It was taking too long. The Yeerks would see the air lock opening. They would see me emerge.

I was almost complete. Only one change remained, and it came last.

My face split open horizontally. A gash. An open wound. Muscles attached themselves to jaw bones. And from those jaw bones grew teeth. How many? Too many to easily count.

The mouth, my mouth opened, shut. Opened, shut again with sudden, savage force.

And then, one last thing. One last change, one last gift from the Blue Blade.

Instinct. The mind that went with the mouth.

The hatch opened. I swam out into the unbounded ocean.

My ocean.

CHAPTER 12
Aximili

I kicked my tail and surged into the water.

How to describe the feeling of the creature's mind beneath and within my own? I sensed no intelligence worth noting. This seemed to me a creature of pure instinct.

The Blue Blade was a creature made up of razored triangles in mind as well as body. The instincts were as clean and elegant as a crystal dagger.

Move. Move. Move.

Kill. Eat.

Move.

And to accomplish these utterly basic ends I discovered a whole array of weapons that had not been visible from the outside.

The Blue Blade had startlingly acute senses. Smell. Hearing. And some new sense, something that seemed to be a sort of electrical field awareness. It was as if every living thing near me was pulsing with a distinct radio emission and I was a receiver.

I heard the Bug fighter. Moved away from it. Fear? No. It was not prey. And there would be no prey near it.

A school of smaller finned creatures passed by, off to my right, running from the Bug fighter. Too small for a meal.

I swam, swam, moved, moved, this way and that, casting about for a scent that would jolt my brain.

WHHUUUMMMPPPPFFF!

A noise that filled the ocean. The part of me that was still Andalite understood. The Yeerks had imploded the dome. It was filling with water, I could hear the bubbles erupting, the tons of seawater rushing in. I could hear the trees snapping like twigs.

No going back. Only forward now.

I swam.

Sounds behind me. Pursuit. Meaningless. I was not pursued. Nothing pursued me. I pursued.

More sounds. The Bug fighter blew past me, rocking me with its wake.

Tseeeeeew!

A blast of energy that set my electrical field senses on fire.

I turned.

Tseeeeeew!

Heat! Irrelevant. Pain! Irrelevant.

I turned and dived.

Tseeeeew!

This time the Dracon beam missed by a larger margin.

They fired again. Sliced part of my tail off. But it was an uneven fight. In the water the Bug fighter was slow in the turns, sluggish. I turned in my own body length.

The Bug fighter dove beneath me. I rose toward the surface. Shadows on the bright barrier of the surface. Something flying low and slow.

Pah-Loosh! Pah-Loosh!

They fell from no great height into the water just fifty feet away. I, the Andalite me, recognized them instantly, though I had never actually seen one except in holographic displays at the academy.

Taxxons.

The only species ever to agree *en masse* to be infested by the Yeerks.

They were large worms. Worms that moved on dozens of sharp, pointed legs set in rows down the lengths of their bloated, vile, pulsating bodies.

I could clearly see the hungry red mouths, the red jelly eyes.

When they lectured us on Taxxons at the academy they emphasized two things: that any Andalite could slaughter an endless number of Taxxons in direct combat. The other thing they emphasized was that if we fell before the Taxxons our fate would be horrifying.

The Taxxons do not accept surrender. They eat the wounded. Even their own.

There were six of the big worms in the water ahead of me. Six arrayed in battle formation against one of me.

I attacked. I raced for the nearest one. The Blue Blade sliced through the water, rolled onto its side, opened its mouth, and dug triangular teeth into too-yielding flesh.

I ripped a two-foot hole in the worm.

"Sreeeeeyah!"

Taxxon blood and organs and bile billowed in the water. Air bubbles seeped from its mouth.

A second Taxxon. Chomp!

A third, a fourth, more, more, more! I was mad with killing rage, slashing, darting, flailing like an insane thing, hitting, biting, ripping, tearing.

Out of control!

The morph had taken over. The creature was directing the action. No, that made it sound as if it was thinking. It thought nothing. Even its low level of intelligence was wiped away, erased by a screaming, demanding urge to massacre anything it could reach.

Six Taxxons were in pieces, floating.

More were dropping into the water, but these new arrivals saw what was happening and swam directly away from me.

No more targets! Nothing left to kill.

I flailed at nothing, bit and slashed the empty water. I would have bitten myself if I could.

And then, suddenly, it was over.

The madness gone, replaced by ice-cold indifference.

I swam away. My Andalite mind regained control. For now.

My first battle. Six Taxxons. And I had learned one thing: If the rest of Earth's species were anything like this Blue Blade, the Yeerks had picked the wrong planet.

CHAPTER 13
Jake

DAY THIRTY-ONE

"Aren't you coming?"

I shrugged. Tom was framed in my bedroom door. He looks a lot like me; at least that's what people say. They always say they can tell we're brothers.

"I wasn't going to," I said. I pointed at the books on my desk. "Homework."

He looked disappointed. "Oh, man, that's too bad, man. I figured you'd be there. There's some people I wanted you to meet. One of the high-up guys in The Sharing is coming."

"Yeah?" I said, trying to sound interested.

"Mr. Visser himself."

I had a sudden mental image . . . a vision, almost. Strange. A picture that had popped into my head. A head without a mouth. Eyes on something like snail stalks.

Whoa. Then it was gone. "Weird name," I said.

"Yeah, well, he's an unusual guy. But very smart. Very cool. Look, who's the homework for? Old Lady Hanna?"

I smiled, despite myself. "Yeah. For Ms. Hanna."

"Tell you what, you come to the meeting with me tonight, I'll guarantee Old Lady Hanna will give you an 'A.' "

"Say what?"

He shrugged. "She's a member, little brother."

"That doesn't mean she'll let me blow off homework," I said.

Tom considered for a moment. He blinked and kind of looked away, almost like he was embarrassed. "No. I don't want you thinking that," he admitted. "Tell you what, though, come to the meeting and I'll help you do the homework when we get home."

Strange having Tom ask me for anything. It was like he was pressuring me. Maybe he was nervous himself and wanted me around as his security blanket.

"Okay," I said. I shut my book.

The phone rang. Tom stepped into the hallway to grab it.

"It's your honey pie," he said.

I flushed. I couldn't control it. I shot him a dark look that just made him laugh. I grabbed the receiver from his hand.

"Hi."

"It's me, Cassie."

"Yeah? Um, hi. What's up?"

"I . . . I, uh, I was wondering if, I don't know . . ."

In the background I heard a voice I knew. Rachel. "Good grief, do I have to do it *for* you?"

"Do you want to study together?" Cassie blurted out in a rush.

"Is Rachel there?" I asked.

"Yes, but she'll be leaving. Sooner than she thinks, if she doesn't watch out."

I sighed. On the scale of things I wanted to do, study with Cassie was about a nine, going to The Sharing was about a one. A minus one. But I'd already told Tom I'd do it.

"Cassie, I really would like to but —"

"Oh! No problem!" she said, too quickly. "I was just, it was only that —"

"Cassie, there is nothing I'd rather do than study with you. Really. Except maybe get some tips from Michael Jordan. But I promised Tom I'd go to this stu . . ." I stopped myself. Tom could be right out in the hall. "This meeting."

"A meeting?"

"Yeah. It's this thing called The Sharing."

Silence.

"Are you there?"

"Yeah."

"Is something the matter?"

"I . . ."

"What is it?"

"I don't know," she said. She sounded confused. Worried. "I don't know. I really don't."

I relaxed a little. Not much. "You know, maybe you're just upset over this thing with Rachel and Marco."

"Over them going out?"

"No, over the whole thing that happened with them. You know, Marco thinking he saw his mom and all. The guys with the guns."

"The *what*?"

I slapped my forehead. "Rachel didn't tell you?"

"Tell me *what*?" Cassie demanded. Then, obviously to Rachel, "*What* didn't Rachel tell me?"

"I thought you'd get all worried," Rachel said in the background.

"Sorry," I said. "Marco hasn't shut up about it, and I just assumed Rachel told you."

"Jake, I have to go and cause Rachel serious bodily pain."

"I understand. Listen, Cassie, how about tomorrow night? I mean, for studying together."

"That would be great."

"Yeah."

"Yeah."

"Go kill Rachel now."

I stepped back out into the hall and hung up the phone. Cool. Cassie, tomorrow night. My insides were churning. Oh, man, what was I going to talk about with her?

Maybe we could talk about why Rachel would keep something secret that Marco wouldn't stop bringing up.

And maybe we could talk about why Cassie got weird when I said the words, "The Sharing."

CHAPTER 14

Tobias

I was used to the place now. I felt comfortable there. Weird feeling. Weird to be comfortable.

I'd been to several meetings of The Sharing. Once some new kids started teasing me, but the real members shut them down fast.

No one gave me any grief at The Sharing. They acted like I was an equal. Like I belonged.

Or at least like I could belong.

Tonight was the night. I had to decide. Join or not. Become a full member or stop coming.

It wasn't that hard a decision for me. What else did I have going on? Where else was I going to go?

And there was another factor.

Two days ago I'd run into Andy and Tap-Tap again. In the gym locker room. There were maybe two dozen other kids in there, so I'd figured I was safe even though this wasn't my regular class and I was only there because I'd missed gym two days in a row. I figured wrong.

They started to stuff me into one of the taller lockers the football team uses. I was yelling, kids were laughing. Not just Andy and Tap-Tap. It was like every kid in there wanted to see me get humiliated.

Then these guys, these two ordinary kids I'd seen at The Sharing, came over. I didn't even know their names. I still don't.

One guy said, "Hey, let him go."

Andy stopped stuffing my face back with his hand. "Are you talking to me?"

"Let him go."

These two Sharing guys didn't have Jake's easy ability to convince people they were serious. But they were determined. The other guy walked over to a weight rack. He picked up about a twenty-pound weight and carried it back to Andy.

"Let him go, or I'll bury this weight in your head."

Andy blinked. Tap-Tap giggled.

Class was changing. New kids were arriving. One of them was Sharing, too. He didn't even ask what was going on. He just moved in beside his two friends. Now it was three of them against Andy and Tap-Tap.

They let me go.

My rescuers didn't even hang around long enough for me to say thanks.

They'd made their point. That's what it meant to be Sharing, not throwing your weight around or anything like some gang or whatever, just the knowledge that there were people backing you up. Looking out for you.

Bill was still my advisor. Only now I was beating him at pool.

"I'm going to do it," I said to him. Then I nailed the four ball.

"Do what? Kick my butt by running the table?"

I laughed. "No. I want to join. I want to be a full member."

He put down his cue, came over, and gave me a sort of arm's-length hug. He held me out to get a good look at me.

"That's cool, Tobias."

"Yeah," I said. I was feeling kind of embarrassed.

"Now, you know this is a big step, right? I mean, we want you to join. We all want you to be a full member. But there are responsibilities that go along with it. It's not just games and fun all the time."

I nodded. "I know. Some Sharing guys saved my rear end the other day. I know what it's about."

"The individual has to give up something to get something in return," he said.

"Yeah. I know. I've been listening to the speeches and all."

"You trade a little bit of freedom for a lot of belonging to something bigger than yourself." He moved closer and lowered his voice to a conspiratorial whisper. "Bigger than you can imagine."

I felt wary. What was he talking about?

"A full member of The Sharing is a special person," Bill said. "A rare and special person." He waved his arm around at the room full of kids and adults. "This is just the surface, Tobias. We are about bigger things. We are going to make this a better world."

"Yeah?"

"Yeah. Change is coming, Tobias. And you'll be part of it. You have no idea. You think you're just some kid, some kid going to school. You have no idea of the untapped potential deep inside yourself. You have no idea what you can become. What you can accomplish."

I nodded like I had some clue. I didn't. But it excited me. Scared me, too, a little. But there was something about The Sharing they don't tell you right at first: You have a few weeks, a month even, but then you have to choose. You can stay and be a full member, or you have to leave.

Leave The Sharing. And do what? Go back to my lovely life?

I spotted Jake. He came in with Tom. Tom gets a lot of respect at the meetings. Even adults are respectful to him.

I caught Jake's eye. He came over to see me. Cool. For once I wasn't running to him like a little puppy dog. He was coming to see me.

"What's up, Tobias?"

I shrugged. "Nothing much. Except I guess tonight is the big night for me."

"Yeah? Why's that?"

"I'm going to become a full member."

He looked at me kind of sideways. "Congratulations, I guess, right?"

"Sure. You should do it, too."

"Uh-huh. That's what Tom keeps telling me."

"So why don't you?" I asked.

He looked uncomfortable. "I don't know. I guess it's just not my thing."

"Oh, you're too cool?"

He looked sharply at me. "I wasn't trying to offend you, man."

"You didn't offend me," I said, sounding offended. "Not at all. I'm just curious. Why don't you want to join? Tom's a member, so it's not like it's just for losers like me."

That came out much harsher and more pathetic than I'd intended.

"Tobias, you're not a loser," he said.

Which just made it worse. It's bad enough being a loser. You don't want the winners like Jake feeling sorry for you.

"Hey, join or not, no problem," I said.

"It's just . . ." He looked down at the floor, then over at Tom who was shaking hands and laughing with a group of guys and girls. "I don't know. People start talking about how the individual has to give way to the group, I just, I don't know. I get kind of . . . jumpy. Besides, how can I join any organization where Mr. Chapman is a member?"

He meant that last part as a joke. But I didn't want to laugh. "Don't you want to be a part of something big and important?"

He shook his head very slightly. "No. I don't want to be 'a part.' Maybe it's just me. Maybe it's just my own mental block. But anytime someone starts talking that stuff, I start looking for the exit door."

"You're a part of lots of things, Jake," I said. "You're part of a team. You're part of your country."

He nodded. "No, I didn't make the team," he said darkly. He forced a happy face. "Hey, I'm just down because of this conversation I had.

Cassie. Kind of bothered me somehow. Not your problem, though. So how about I say congratulations, and wish you luck and all."

"Okay. Cool."

"Yeah."

CHAPTER 15
Tobias

There were four of us slated to become full members. There was a police officer named Edward. There was a newspaper reporter named Kiko. There was a guy who managed local bands. His name was Barry.

And then, there was me.

Why me? The question was impossible to avoid. How did I fit into this group? Was it really true that The Sharing didn't care if you were young or old, male, female, black, white, Asian, Christian, Jew, Muslim, Buddhist, atheist, straight, gay, rich, or poor?

I mean, that's what they said. But lots of people say that. They don't always mean it.

Mostly people look for ways to treat other people like dirt.

They put us in a small room, dimly lit. Like a dentist's waiting room only with mood lighting and no magazines. There was the door we came in. And a door that hadn't opened yet.

I looked at the others. Edward and Kiko paid no attention to me. Barry nodded. They must have been wondering what some kid was doing there. Adults have an automatic prejudice against kids. They never take kids seriously, even when they pretend to. At least that's my experience.

I said hi to Barry.

"Hi, kid. What's your name?"

"Tobias."

"Good name. You like music?"

"Sure."

"Ever hear of Format Cee's Colon?"

I shook my head. He looked disappointed. "Yeah, well, you will. Next big thing. You heard it here, first. They just need a break. We've got a video, but we can't get any play on MTV."

I nodded like I cared. "I guess you need that, huh?"

"Absolutely. They say they can help."

"Who?"

"The Sharing. Who else?"

"Ah."

The door opened. The door that hadn't opened before. Mr. Chapman. Our vice principal at school. So far my meetings with Mr. Chapman had been in his office. Him asking me to tell him who had beat me up. Or who had pantsed me and shoved me into the girls' bathroom. And me refusing to tell.

"Kiko?" Chapman said.

She jerked to her feet. Straightened her trim skirt. Chapman gave me a friendly wink and led Kiko away.

Barry fell silent. He was nervous.

The policeman wasn't in uniform, but I knew he was a cop. My uncle has been arrested a couple of times in his life and cops are the one thing he really gets passionate about. He's always pointing them out. So I know a policeman when I see one.

Basically, I figured if my uncle hated them, they were probably all right. It set my mind at ease a little seeing him there. I mean, if he was joining it had to be okay. Right?

The door opened again and I jerked involuntarily.

It was Bill. "Hey, switch to decaf, man," he joked.

"Sorry."

"Let's go."

I stood up. Barry gave me a nod of encouragement. The cop just stared blankly ahead of him.

I walked through the door.

Bill led me down a hallway. Suddenly, in the middle of the hallway he stopped and gave me a mysterious look. He pressed his hand against a small rectangular panel set about chest-high.

Suddenly a door appeared. It opened on darkness.

We stepped through. Not completely dark. There was a red light. Metal stairs, leading down.

I hesitated. Bill laughed. "Don't worry, it's just a bit of melodrama."

Down. Not far. Three flights. To a landing, and another door, and another hallway. Another door.

Open. Inside, a table. Six chairs. Chapman sat at the head of the table. Beside him, imperious, impatient, almost menacing, was the man who had spoken at the meeting earlier. Mr. Visser.

Kiko sat to Chapman's right. She smiled at me. A weird smile. The side of her face spasmed suddenly, but then she was smiling again.

In one corner was a sort of metal tub. Like the whirlpools the football team uses. Stainless steel, just big enough for one person. There was some sort of harness or whatever on the lip of the tub, and a steel chair.

"Tobias," Chapman said.

"Yes, sir?"

"Bill tells us that you are ready to become a full member of The Sharing."

I nodded.

"Why do you wish to join us?"

I shrugged. "Because . . . I . . . because you know, what they're always talking about. What Mr. Visser was saying. Being part of something greater than myself. Part of something big."

Chapman glanced at Mr. Visser. Nervously, I thought.

Mr. Visser took a deep breath. "Is all this necessary?"

Chapman said, "Receptivity is helpful, Visser. There is less chance of . . . of problems later."

"Yes, yes, but get on with it."

Chapman forced his features back into a pleasant smile. "Are you ready, Tobias? Is this what you truly want?"

What I wanted? I wanted to fly. To spread my wings, catch the breeze, feel my talons leave the branch, soar as the thermal raised me up to the clouds.

What?

Bill nudged me. "Yes," I said.

"And you will surrender yourself to The Sharing?"

"Yes." The image had been so strong. So real.

Flying high, seeing through eyes that were like telescopes.

Chapman nodded to Bill. Bill held my shoulders from behind and guided me to the whirlpool thing.

"Sit there," he said.

I sat. The chair was cold. The surface of the liquid in the tub was still. Dark. Heavy-looking, as if it maybe wasn't water.

No big deal, I told myself. *Lots of organizations have weird initiations and stuff. No problem.* But I felt off now. The vision, what was it? Some desperate fantasy?

"Place your right hand here," Bill said.

I placed my hand in what could only be a shackle. A handcuff. My insides were churning now. I was placing myself totally in their power. What was I doing? What was I doing?

Bill fastened the cuff.

"Now your left hand."

No, no, this was insane. No, this was wrong. No. No. Handcuffs? I looked pleadingly at Mr. Chapman. He was the vice principal, he wouldn't be part of anything bad, would he?

But Mr. Visser was in the way. It was his bored face I saw.

I placed my left hand. Bill fastened the cuff.

"Now lay your head down, sideways, in the harness," Bill instructed.

"What is this?" I asked. "What are you doing? I mean, what's going to happen?"

"Your whole world is going to change, Tobias," Bill said soothingly. "You will see and know and understand *everything*."

"I don't think I . . ." I couldn't breathe. A voice in my head was screaming, *Run! Run!* My mind was reeling. "I think I changed my mind."

Bill suppressed a smile. "You want to leave The Sharing? You want to leave all of us? All your friends? After all we've done for you? Okay, Tobias. But what will you do, then? Where will you go? What's your future?"

My heart was pounding. "I don't know," I said desperately. "I just . . . I . . ."

"There is no 'I,' Tobias. What are you? One lonely, messed-up kid. No one loves you. No one cares. No one but us. Put your head in the harness."

I shook my head, wildly, firmly. "No. No. I don't want to do this."

Bill smiled. He laughed. "Well, guess what? It's too late."

He grabbed my head in his two hands and shoved it down.

"No! Mr. Chapman! No!"

Chapman got up and came over. He helped force me down. I was screaming, crying, yelling now. Helpless. My hands held firm.

"Let me go! Let me go! Let me go!"

The harness was closed over my neck, around my head. I couldn't move it. I could barely move my mouth to beg for mercy.

Bill and Chapman stepped back. There was a whirring motor somewhere close. The side of my head was forced down toward the surface of the liquid.

"No! No! No!"

"You see, in the end we have to use force," Mr. Visser said.

"True, Visser, but we only have this problem in twenty-one percent of the cases of willing members. And there are sixty-four percent fewer incidents of contested control with voluntary hosts."

"I know the statistics," Mr. Visser snapped. "Just do it. I have thirty minutes left before I have to demorph."

I heard all this like it was coming from far away. I listened hoping to hear some note of mercy, some sense that maybe this was all a terrible joke, a hazing, something.

My ear touched the water.

A moment later, something touched my ear.

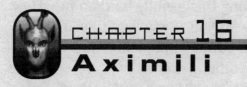

CHAPTER 16
Aximili

"Look, son, I just want to try and help you. But I can't help you if you don't talk to me."

I had lived on the surface of planet Earth for several days. I had accomplished some things. I had observed that a species called humans were the dominant life-form. This had taken some time.

For one thing, I wanted to guard against the problem of cultural prejudice. Coming from a relatively large species myself, I tended naturally to look first to species that were of a similar size.

I didn't want to be a victim of my own expectations. So I deliberately investigated a number of other fairly ubiquitous species. But none of those species possessed even rudimentary technology.

I considered a species called cows. In places they were numerous. But despite their superficial similarity to my own species, I determined that they were not highly intelligent.

"You're making this awfully hard on me. How can I prescribe for you if you won't even talk to me? I know you can communicate. You've communicated with other patients."

"Yesssss," I said. "I can communicate. Cate-uh. I can-nuh com-yew-yew-nicate. Is it not time for cookies?"

In the end it became clear that my first instinct was correct: Humans were the dominant species.

I had acquired a human morph. And I had learned to pass as a human. In fact, I had been asked — forcefully — to adopt a particular location as my primary residence.

"You have to at least give me your name."

"I am called Hey Moron. Hey! Moron-nuh!"

The human before me closed his eyes and used his five-fingered hand to rub the flesh stretched across his forehead. Then he rubbed the back of his neck. Then he exhaled breath through his mouth. He was called Dr. Duberstein. Early in my stay at this location I had not fully understood his function. Now I did.

"That's not exactly a name. That's just something someone called you."

"Ah. When will I receive ree-seeeve the cookies-zuh? They are delicious, mmm-mmm."

"Well, to tell you the truth, the nurses don't want you around at cookie time. You made quite a scene yesterday."

This was disturbing news. "No cookies?"

He shook his head back and forth and looked at me with his two small eyes located on the front of his face. "No cookies."

"Then I must go elsewhere in search of cookies," I said. "The cookies formed by two thin, round, black discs with a layer of adhesive white substance between them are the finest accomplishment of your species!"

"*My* species?"

I had made a mistake. I had allowed my agitation over the cookies to cause me to be careless. This was not the time to reveal myself.

Humans use their mouths for eating — much as the Blue Blade — which I learned the humans call a shark. But humans possess an incredible sense that goes beyond anything the shark could boast: taste.

Taste! And such tastes! Cigarette butts, baloney sandwiches, grape juice, Vaseline, and best of all, the indescribably vibrant, mind-altering, overwhelming taste of cookies!

Especially the cookies formed by two thin, round, black discs with a layer of adhesive white substance between. Someday I hope my fellow Andalites will be able to visit Earth and morph to human simply for the intense pleasure to be had from eating cookies with a mouth.

"I meant *our* species."

"You said *your* species."

"Evidently I am insane. May I go now?"

The human raised his hands vertically and said, "Why me, Lord? Why?"

I left the small room and went back out into the larger room where numerous humans wandered back and forth holding discussions using mouth-sounds. At first I had assumed that these discussions were being transmitted by some sort of very small communications link since they were addressed to persons who were not in evidence.

Later I understood this, as well.

The humans had various names. Two of them were named Elvis Presley. One was named John. He was the one who had first witnessed me demorphing.

It was an accident. I'd hidden within a small enclosed area used for voiding biological wastes. But John had caught me. He had seen me in my natural state.

He had seemed unsurprised.

John told one of the nurses that I was an alien. And for a moment I was quite concerned. But the nurse seemed bored by this fact. And it seems that many of the residents of this particular group habitation are aliens.

It took me several days before it occurred to me that the humans in this group were not entirely like the broader spectrum of humans. They suffered from mental illnesses. But, on balance they seemed less aggressive and hostile than the humans portrayed on the two-dimensional audio-visual display screen called a TV.

So I stayed with them. But now, if there were no more cookies, I would clearly have to leave. In any case, it was time for me to be about my primary mission. Whatever that was.

I waited till darkness, when the orderlies turn out the lights and the first Elvis Presley sings an awful musical composition about a place called Heartbreak Hotel.

I demorphed. I used my tail blade to slice open the steel wire mesh that covered the windows.

I was out in Earth's night, wiser about humans, and about cookies, but no closer to finding an answer to Elfangor's fate. Or a way home.

Humans lacked the technology for Zero-space

travel. Their spacecraft was laughable explosive devices used to propel satellites into orbit. They were centuries away from Z-space travel.

Which left me just two possibilities: One was to hope that some Andalites survived and were present on Earth.

The other possibility was only very slightly more likely: the Yeerks.

Were the Yeerks on Earth? I didn't know. I knew that they were in orbit. I knew that they had located the sunken Dome ship. But were they engaged in a conquest of Earth?

And if they were, what were the odds that I could steal a Bug fighter and escape?

I needed a plan. I needed to learn whether the Yeerks were here. But how?

How? TV.

I had come to understand at least some aspects of human technology, in particular their communications technology. They have telephones, which communicate only the spoken mouth-sounds of their primary communication. They have an inexplicable artifact of which they are absurdly proud called the Internet, which is evidently meant to be a sort of adjunct to other, more effective technologies. They have books, of course, models of efficiency. And they have TV.

TV is immediate, pervasive, and transmits sound, images, and text.

In my time at the residence for insane humans I had learned to locate structures within the gridwork of streets. I knew the location of a television studio. And I knew at what time they would begin a “live” broadcast of news.

My method of discovering whether the Yeerks had infiltrated the human species was quite simple: Show them an Andalite.

CHAPTER 17
Tobias

I felt it enter my ear.

I've never felt anything like it. It wasn't that it was painful. It wasn't, not really. But something was crawling *into* my ear. Into my ear.

"No! No! No! Help me, someone help me! Mr. Chapman, you have to . . . Bill, help me!"

It wasn't stopping. It kept writhing, forcing itself into my head. I could feel it through a numbness. I could feel it inside my ear, deeper, oh God, in my head!

"Let me go. I'll do anything you want. Let me go! Please, please."

Deeper.

Then . . .

Then I felt the first tingling sensation of a new

presence. A mind. It was . . . I didn't hear it, didn't see it, but it was there, there and touching my own thoughts.

Suddenly my hands, which had been clenched in rage, relaxed. The fingers hung limp.

I felt a chill. Cold as death.

No. It couldn't be.

All at once memories were spilling out. Like I was thinking back over my life, only I wasn't. I wasn't, I didn't want to. I was sitting there, standing, hovering, I don't know where I was, but I was there watching as my memories were replayed at hyper speed, tumbling, spilling out.

My mouth said, "I have him."

My mouth had moved! Lips, tongue, throat, all had worked to form words I didn't mean to say.

"Let me up, this is rather uncomfortable," my mouth said.

My voice! I heard my own voice with my own ears but I hadn't spoken. Had I? Was I losing my mind?

"Report," Mr. Visser said.

Only he wasn't *Mr. Visser*. He was Visser Three. Not a human at all. An alien.

Okay, this was all a dream. This was all not happening. None of it. Aliens called Yeerks who infested other species?

Insane! I was dreaming or something.

My mouth said, "Odret-One-Seven-Seven, of the Culat Hesh pool. Reporting for duty."

A Yeerk. In my brain. In my brain, scanning my memories, moving my mouth, rubbing my chafed wrists, stretching my fear-strained back.

All of them, it's what they all were. Chapman, Bill, Tom, all the full members. Them, and thousands more. Policemen, politicians, newspeople, businessmen, teachers, writers. And kids.

Why kids? Because kids are never suspected. They can be used anywhere.

I tried to look at Chapman. But I couldn't move my eyes! I wanted to scream. But my mouth, my vocal cords, it was like being paralyzed. Paralyzed and no one even to know that I was there, frozen, frozen inside my own body.

Out of the corner of eyes I could no longer aim, I saw Bill smirk. He leaned close. "I know you can still hear me, Tobias. Now do you see what I meant? You have to give something up human, to be a part of something larger."

He laughed.

But Visser Three snapped, "Shut up, fool. Get out."

Bill disappeared from the room. Fast. Very fast.

"All right, Odret-One-Seven-Seven, you have your human host," Visser Three said. "Now, what orders do you bring from the Council of Thirteen?"

The Yeerk in my head, I could see his thoughts. Not all, but enough. I knew he was wary of Visser Three. But not frightened. This Yeerk was under the protection of another power.

But not the Council of Thirteen! He had lied to Visser Three. Or at least twisted the truth.

"The council congratulates you on taking command of the Earth invasion," my mouth said. "The council wishes you to know that your request to alter the tactics established by Visser One is denied. Earth will be taken by infiltration and subversion. It will not be openly attacked."

Visser One. Yes, Odret was her ally. Visser One was Visser Three's enemy. She had been the first Yeerk on planet Earth. She had discovered the planet and launched the invasion.

But Odret was leery even of Visser One. She told some story of being instantaneously transported from her ship to a museum on the planet. It made no sense to Odret.

Visser Three had begun to demorph. He was becoming an Andalite. The Yeerk inside me, in my head, the slug creature who had wrapped himself around my brain and gained total control of me, knew about Andalites.

They were the enemy. Duplicitous, hypocritical, sanctimonius, deadly, and dangerous. Visser

Three had the only Andalite host body in all the Yeerk Empire. The Andalite in question was morph-capable.

It made Visser Three very dangerous. Odret was worried. And Odret was confused. He did not understand why Visser One opposed using greater force against the humans.

That was not his concern, he told himself. His concern was to stay alive. To do so he — I — had to obey Visser Three while pretending to obey the Council of Thirteen and avoid so angering Visser Three that his life would end in hideous torture.

My life, my very mind, everything that was me, had been stolen. Stolen by a creature who was almost certainly doomed.

Bill came back into the room, rushing. "Visser! On the TV! Right now!"

<What, you idiot?>

"An Andalite."

CHAPTER 18
Jake

"Look, Tom, it's just not me, okay?"

"Yeah, whatever," Tom said. He was mad. He was hurt. He felt like I was rejecting him. "It's just that tonight was kind of special, with Mr. Visser being there and all. I mean, right now probably your friend Tobias is becoming a full member. He's probably already one of us."

"That's good for him. And for you," I said. I was losing my patience. The whole thing was giving me the willies. "But you know what? The more you pressure me, the less I'm interested."

We got home. Tom slammed in through the front door. I slammed through behind him. I didn't need this. Just because I didn't want to join some stupid club. I had homework to do. I'd passed up a chance to be with Cassie.

"Besides, he's not my friend," I said to Tom's retreating back. "He's just some guy from school."

My mom was in the kitchen paying bills. She had the TV on as background noise. The local news.

I entered in search of junk food. Tom started to take off upstairs, then I guess he reconsidered. He flopped down in the family room and snapped on the TV. Some game was on.

"Hey, Mom, what's up?" I said.

"The electric bill," she muttered. "What the . . . What is going on, is that some kind of gag?"

I followed the direction of her amazed stare. It was the familiar news set with the familiar newspeople.

But standing in front of them was something decidedly unfamiliar.

It was a centaur. No, not a centaur. Not like it was half-horse and half-human, more like it was half-muscular blue deer, half-human. Only with a face that was definitely not human. For a start, it had no mouth. But it had two additional eyes mounted on moveable stalks atop its head.

And it had a tail like a python with a blade at the end.

"Special effects," I said. "It must be for some movie or whatever."

"Tom!" my mom called. "Turn on channel seven." Then, to me, "I don't think the anchors expected this. They look scared to death."

I shot a look toward Tom, illuminated by the glow of the TV in the family room. He was standing up. Rigid. Staring. But not amazed or amused or curious.

His face was a mask of rage and hatred.

The TV screen went blank. Up came a still shot saying *Sorry, we are experiencing technical difficulties.*

"That was weird," my mom said.

"Yeah," I agreed. But I was watching Tom. His fists were clenched. He bolted for the stairs and took them two steps at a time.

"You want some chicken? There's some in the fridge."

"No. Thanks," I said. I headed for the stairs. I didn't know why. I crept up them, moving as silently as I could.

At the top of the stairs I paused, measuring my breath, quieting my heart.

". . . I saw," Tom said into the receiver.

I waited. Hugged the wall.

"It will take ten minutes —"

I peeked around the corner. Tom yanked the

receiver from his ear. Someone was screaming abusively. I could hear the sound if not the words.

"Immediately!" Tom said and dropped the phone. He ran into his room and came out a few seconds later. He was shoving something into his waistband up under his jean jacket.

It was impossible to avoid thinking it was a gun. I walked past him, pretending not to notice. He grabbed me. Pushed me against the wall.

"I have to go out. Cover for me. If Mom or Dad asks, I'm studying. Got it?"

I nodded. It wasn't so different from any number of times Tom had playfully put on a similar act. We both knew not to take it seriously. Just one problem: This time Tom was deadly serious.

CHAPTER 19
Jake

Wherever Tom was going he'd have to take my mom's car. He wasn't thinking clearly if he thought I could cover for that. My dad wasn't home yet and when he got home he'd see my mom's car was out. How was I supposed to explain that?

Besides, this was bigger than some concern over getting grounded. Tom was into something dangerous.

If he was going to avoid being seen by my mom he'd have to take the stairs down to the basement then go out that way. That gave me about five seconds' lead time.

I slid my bedroom window up and shinnied out onto the pitched roof. Rolled down, checked to make sure I was on the right side of the fence separating front and backyards, grabbed the gutter, and prayed it would hold my weight.

I dropped to the ground and ran to the back door of the garage. The automatic garage door around the front was just starting to rise.

I popped the back door of the minivan, jumped in, cursed myself for making the springs bounce, pulled the door down, and went fetal behind the back row of seats.

I heard the driver's-side door open and slam. The key, the engine. We squealed out of the driveway. Fishtailed onto the road and blew through the subdivision at three times the speed limit.

I knew where we were heading. Knew it in my bones. We were heading for channel seven. Too much coincidence for anything else.

And Tom was armed.

What was I supposed to do? What *could* I do? Only one thing was sure: I had to stop Tom before he got himself in some kind of serious trouble. He was my big brother and he was supposed to protect me. But that had to go both ways if he was the one who was in trouble.

A gun? Did Tom really have a gun? The idea made me sick. Who owned handguns? Criminals. Pathetic people who thought it would make them important. Nuts.

One thing was for sure. If my parents found

out they'd go nuclear. My parents didn't spank, and anyway Tom was way too old. But if they learned he had a gun, Tom was going to live out the rest of his years till his eighteenth birthday locked in his room having his food shoved in under the door.

What was he doing?

A siren! The cops. Thank God. They'd pull him over. They'd slow him down at least, writing him a ticket.

The siren was right behind us. I could see red flashing lights swirling against the seat back. I rose cautiously to peek out. Just as I did the police car turned off its siren and lights.

The cops pulled around us, revving their big engine, and started the siren again.

They were escorting us! We blew through red lights, through stop signs, jerked into oncoming traffic.

Wait a minute, was Tom some kind of undercover cop or something? Insane. Stupid. He was in high school.

Suddenly the cop car screeched to a halt. Crouched down I could see the big blue-and-white channel seven logo.

Slam!

I opened the door, slid out cautiously. Tom was running up the front steps of the four-story station building. Two cops were right with him.

Both had guns drawn. And Tom . . . Tom was armed as well. Only it wasn't like any gun I'd ever seen.

Absurd, I thought. Ridiculous. It was all part of some elaborate practical joke. Had to be. Because otherwise, the only other explanation was that my big brother was carrying some kind of ray gun.

They shoved through the smoked-glass doors into a dimly lit lobby, already looking like a business shut down for the night. I grabbed a side door, just off to the right.

There was a uniformed security guard fretting nervously, obviously not sure what to do.

"Hey, glad you're here," the guard said. "There's some kind of a, I don't even know what it is, but it's in the —"

Tseeeew!

I jerked in surprise. A bright red lance of light had shot from Tom's weapon.

The guard fell back. There was smoke billowing from his uniform.

I yelled. Not a word, just a yell of surprise and shock and horror.

Tom spun. He peered at me through the gloom. He fired.

Tseeew!

Miss!

No! He'd shot at me. He'd shot at me! Did he even know it was me? Had he recognized me?

One of the cops aimed.

BLAM! BLAM! BLAM! BLAM!

The glass behind me shattered and fell in a hail of shards. The cop emptied his gun. But I was hugging the floor and crawling behind a display bearing artwork. Paintings. Photographs.

The firing stopped. Holes had been blown through the pictures.

By the time I worked up nerve to look again, they were all three gone.

I couldn't breathe. My heart was hammering like it was trying to bang its way out of my chest.

A ray gun. A laser or whatever. Just like Marco and Rachel. Marco would think I made it all up to top his story.

If I lived long enough to tell him.

I heard screams from some other part of the building. I heard the strange "tseeew" sound of the laser beam or whatever it was.

What could I do? I wasn't armed. I wasn't some action hero. All I could do was hide. Hide right here, right where I was, till the cops showed up. Only the cops were already here.

So I hid. For half an hour I just crouched, waiting for it all to end.

But then . . . then something started to happen to me. My hands were changing, flattening out. And orange-and-black fur was growing. And my fingernails were extending, curving, forming claws!

What was happening to me? What was happening?

Then, instantly, my hands were normal again. Stress. That was it. I was imagining things. Freaking.

Losing my mind.

There came the sound of yelling, loud protests, cries of rage and fear.

I peeked again from behind my flimsy protection. I looked through a bullet hole that had made an extra eye for a portrait of a woman.

A dozen guys, all armed, some with guns, some with the laser gun things, were herding seven handcuffed people between them. The anchorpeople were among them, makeup turning their faces orange.

Tom was there, calmly supervising.

Through the smoked glass I could see a limousine pull up. My assistant principal, Mr. Chapman, stepped out and held the door for Mr. Visser, the guy from The Sharing.

And then, last to step from the car, was Tobias.

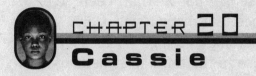

CHAPTER 20
Cassie

DAY THIRTY-THREE

Jake wouldn't talk in my house. He was too jumpy. So we went out to the barn.

It was Saturday morning. No school. And my dad was at Home Depot buying materials for some improvements in the barn. He'd be gone for hours.

Rachel showed up about ten minutes later with Marco. Jake had called them.

Jake didn't waste time. "I was shot at," he said.

Marco had just sat down on a hay bale. He jumped back up. "Okay, what is this? Are you goofing on Rachel and me?"

"No." Jake had a look I'd never seen before.

There was not the slightest hint of lightheartedness in his expression. He was serious. Grim, even. He seemed older.

"I was shot at. With guns. And with some kind of laser. Just like you two."

Weird. Once again, I had this weird feeling. *Déjà vu.* The sense that we'd all been here, together. Not once, but many times. Only . . . only there was something missing.

My eyes rose to the rafters. Something missing.

"What is this?" Rachel exploded. "Someone has a grudge against us? What did we ever do?" She peered at Jake. "We're cousins, does this have something to do with that?"

Marco flopped back on the hay bale. Like he did sometimes. Like he'd done so many times. And yet never done. He'd never been in our barn before.

Jake shook his head. "I don't think it has to do with us directly. Marco says he saw his mom. Only she's dead." He saw Marco flinch. "Sorry, man."

"Yeah. But it was her. Look, you know me, Jake, you've known me my entire life practically. Have I ever hallucinated? Have I ever seen something that wasn't there?"

Jake shook his head. "No. You are probably

the last person on earth who'd imagine something like that."

"She was there," Marco said. "I just don't know how. And I don't know why she wouldn't stop. I mean, any answer I come up with sounds like something you'd hear in a conspiracy chat room. I don't believe that stuff. I don't think the big corporations or the mafia or the CIA or little green men from Mars or whatever are secretly controlling our lives. That's crazy, wack-job stuff. But what am I supposed to think when I see my mom, and I chase after her, and these guys end up shooting at Rachel and me?"

"With laser beams," Rachel added. She was pacing back and forth, an almost funny reflection of a recovering raccoon behind her that was pacing its cage.

Jake nodded. He seemed like he wanted to say something, but he was hesitating.

"What is it?" I asked him.

"Maybe *I'm* a crazy wack-job," he said. "I . . . I think maybe there is a conspiracy."

Rachel stopped pacing. "Say what?"

Jake sighed. "I was following Tom. This thing happened on TV, on the news. Suddenly there's this alien-looking thing. Very weird. Kind of cool. Anyway, I'm thinking it's some kind of publicity thing. But Tom is freaking out. Like eight seconds later he's grabbed my mom's car and he's tearing out of there. I stash in the backseat. He goes straight for the TV studio. And he has a gun."

"Whoa! Tom had a gun?" Rachel demanded. "Did you tell your parents?"

"It's past that," Jake said. "At the TV station, he shot someone. Two cops were with him. They helped him. They shot at me, only they didn't know it was me. They grabbed everyone at the station and hustled them out of there, and Tom was in charge. And by the way? The gun he had?"

"Don't even say ray gun," Rachel said.

"What are you even *talking* about?" Marco said. "I thought my story was bizarre."

"Tom and the cops dragged those people out of there in handcuffs. These famous newspeople and all. Then Chapman showed up."

"Chapman? *Chapman* Chapman? Our Chapman?"

"Yeah. And this guy named Mr. Visser. And Tobias. You know, the kid who was hanging with us for a while? They're all there, too."

Marco said, "Why? Why them? Tom, Chapman, Tobias. Mr. Whatever? The cops?"

Jake shook his head slowly. "I don't even want to say this, but Tom, Chapman, Mr. Visser, and Tobias are all members of The Sharing."

"Aren't they just like some family thing or whatever?" Rachel asked.

Jake nodded. "So they claim. But it's kind of a big coincidence."

"How about this alien thing you saw on TV?" Marco asked.

"What about it?"

He shrugged. "What'd it look like?"

"I don't know, like a —"

"Like a blue deer," I said. "Only it had a kind of human face. And a long tail."

Jake looked at me in surprise. "You saw it on TV, too?"

"No." I shook my head. "No. I've never seen it. But I know that it has two eyes on top of its head, on these little stalks."

No one moved. The three of them just stared at me.

"And I'll tell you something else. He should be here." I pointed to a spot off to one side. My arm was goose-bumped all the way up and down. "He should be standing right there."

CHAPTER 21

Cassie

"There's something wrong," I said.

"Do you think? There's plenty wrong," Rachel said. "Marco and I get shot at. Jake gets shot at. We got some kind of cult. My cousin has a ray gun and is shooting it while cops stand around and do nothing. Marco's mom is walking around alive, wearing a wig."

Jake came over and took my hand and bent down to look into my eyes. It was so sweet. And I so needed it.

"Cassie, what do you mean?" Jake asked.

I felt wetness on my cheeks. Why was I crying? I was the only one who hadn't been shot at so far.

"I thought I was going nuts," I said. "Ever

since, I don't know, for weeks I've had this feeling deep down inside that things weren't right. There's supposed . . ." I let go of Jake and threw up my hands. "I can't explain it. Just that everything is wrong. This alien, I heard him talking, kind of, only he was out in the water somewhere. And I have these dreams, these amazing dreams where I'm not me, I'm an animal. A bug sometimes and I'm scared. Or a wolf. Or a bird."

I spotted Marco rolling his eyes. I also spotted Rachel sending him a "keep your mouth shut" look.

But Jake looked at his hands like he'd never seen them before. "Or a tiger," he whispered to himself.

And once more I was drawn to look up. Up at a particular spot in the rafters. "Just now I had the feeling that someone was missing. Two someones. The alien is one. He's supposed to be here. And . . . and I know this sounds crazy . . ."

"Noooo, sounds perfectly sensible to me," Marco said not-quite-under-his-breath.

". . . there's supposed to be a bird. A big one. Right up there. Anyway. Anyway, just now when you said Mr. Visser, I got this chill. He's . . . somehow he's part of it, too."

"Where are Mulder and Scully?" Marco wondered.

Jake nodded, like he half-believed. But he

looked away, too, like you do when someone says something crazy. "You had a bad feeling from the start about The Sharing."

Pity. Great.

Rachel had this angry-concerned look, like she didn't know what to say or do to help me out, but she'd gladly yell at anyone who gave me any trouble.

I'd just spilled my guts. And the result was that the three of them, including my best friend and the guy I liked more than ever, were all thinking I needed to see a shrink.

"Oh, man," I said. "I am losing it, aren't I?"

To my surprise it was Marco who came to my defense, in his own way. "Yeah, you are losing it. You're crazy. Insane. Nuts. The only thing crazier than what you said is some guy who thinks that his big brother, the assistant principal, and Tobias the Mega Dweeb are shooting up a TV studio. And the only thing crazier than that is some kid who thinks his dead mom is running around town with laser-shooting bodyguards."

"We have to do something," Rachel said decisively.

"Do what?" I asked her.

"I don't know. Something. There really is some kind of conspiracy. I mean, what are we supposed to do, just do nothing?"

Marco said, "Rachel, what are the four of us going to do?"

"I don't know!" she yelled in frustration. "Something! Jake? What do we do?"

"Yeah. What do we do, Big Jake?" Marco asked, half-mocking.

"What do you mean, what do we do?" Jake shot back. "Why are you asking me?"

Marco shrugged. "You're the leader, man."

"What are you talking about? The leader of what? And why am I the leader?"

"Because you are," I said. The words were out of my mouth before I could think about them. I felt as if . . . as if I was a judge and had just passed sentence on Jake.

Marco jerked his thumb at me. "What the crazy chick said: Because you *are*."

Jake looked at Rachel, dumbfounded. Rachel looked at me. An eerie look. Like she was listening to me talk, only I wasn't saying anything.

Then Rachel said, "What do we do, Jake?"

For a long minute it felt as if the entire barn was frozen. The three of us looked at Jake. He looked back at us, each in turn, this helpless, almost hopeless look on his face.

And then he said, "We have to find out what's going on. We start with Tom. He's the obvious target."

Jake. Decisive, once the moment for decision arrived.

"Let's grab him, tie him down, threaten to give him up to the FBI unless he tells us what's up," Rachel said.

Rachel, bold, ready to act regardless of consequences.

"If he really shot someone, Tom's dangerous," Marco disagreed. "Which means whatever we do has to be subtle. If there's some kind of conspiracy involving The Sharing, we're not going to know if anyone we talk to is hooked up with them. We need proof before we make a move."

Marco, cautious and clever.

A chill crawled up my spine. I felt as if the universe had just shifted. Like . . . like for weeks I'd been riding a bike with the chain always slipping. And like the chain had just caught again.

Things weren't right. Not right. But more right than they'd been since we'd left the mall together.

CHAPTER 22
Tobias

DAY THIRTY-FOUR

I was helpless. Powerless. Unable to move an eye. Unable to lift a finger. Unable to speak. Unable to alter a facial expression. To smile. Frown. Give any sign that I was alive within my own body, a captive inside my own brain.

I had watched, helpless to cry out, as the Yeerks had dragged the poor men and women from the channel seven studio into vans. Had driven them at breakneck speed toward a water tower that concealed a secret entrance to the vast underground complex of the Yeerk pool.

I'd been unable to cry out in horror as one by one they were dragged, kicking and crying and begging, down the steel pier. The Hork-Bajir-Controllers had held them tight and kicked them to their knees, and shoved the heads down into that seething cesspool.

Every one of them was infested. Every one would now agree on the same cover story to explain away the odd appearance of the blue-furred alien. No charges would be filed. The guard Tom had shot survived, but would never be free. He was infested in his hospital bed. I was there, observing.

And now I was in my room. At home. Odret was still playing the role of Tobias. Still being me.

Odret, the Yeerk, was growing ever more nervous. I could sense his emotions at times. Sometimes he would sift through my memories, looking for a thrill, an escape. Like someone scanning the shelves at Blockbuster, looking for a movie to take his mind off his troubles.

I had to laugh, down in my corner of powerlessness. Odret had the wrong host if he wanted a lot of good times.

He was nervous because of Visser Three. The visser was not behaving as he should, somehow. It wasn't anything obvious. More a question of something missing.

For one thing, Visser Three had a reputation. He was notoriously volatile. He would blow up over very little. But he was treating Odret with elaborate courtesy. Allowing Odret access to anything and everything. Not even making an effort to conceal disasters like the sudden appearance of an Andalite.

Why?

<What a pathetic life you've led, Tobias,> Odret said to me.

<I guess I have.>

<I find nothing in your memories worth seeing again. Nothing was worth seeing a first time.>

<Well, that's how it is, right? The Sharing is a magnet for losers. They go for the weak. So what did you expect?>

To say that I hated myself would be an understatement. Odret had rifled through my memories, each more embarrassing than the one before. I'd had to relive too many things I had tried to forget.

Most painful of all was the image of myself swallowing everything The Sharing told me. I had walked, willingly, to my own destruction. At the time I'd seen no alternative. Now I saw nothing but alternatives.

Was my home a dreary, awful place? Yes. Was I somehow marked as a bully magnet? Yes. Was I different, strange, not-quite-normal? Yes.

And to fight all of that I had destroyed myself. Brilliant, Tobias. Brilliant. All of life's pains combined could not have equaled what I now endured.

Even now no easy answers leaped to mind. I could not easily have stood the bullying. I could not easily have survived the loneliness. In my fantasies I could construct fantastic escapes, but in reality there was no easy way. My life was non-fiction, not some story where the endings are always happy. I couldn't simply become a different person. I couldn't just have some great insight that would save me from myself.

All I could have done, really, was wait. I could have endured. I saw that now. It wasn't a dramatic answer. Wasn't exactly inspiring.

Endure. Outlast. Outwait.

I might have been able to do that. I'm not a fool, I know that school was just a part of my life. You spend eighteen years as a kid, then maybe seventy years as an adult. And what you are as a kid isn't what you'll be as an adult, not always, anyway.

Endure. I could have done that.

Now, too late. My nose itched. I could not scratch it.

Odret checked the clock. He got up, moved my legs and arms, aimed my eyes. I walked past my uncle.

"Where do you think you're going?"

"Out," my mouth said.

"Not if I say you don't!" he yelled.

I/we ignored him. Out the door. A car appeared. I waited for it, impatient. Odret was hungry. He needed Kandrona rays. He needed to feed in the Yeerk pool.

The car drove us to McDonald's. We went in, went up to the counter and gave the counter girl there a code word. Ten minutes later I stepped off the last stair and into the Yeerk pool complex.

I walked self-importantly toward the first pier. Two Hork-Bajir were standing guard, checking people off on a sort of palm-top computer.

"Odret-One-Seven-Seven," my mouth said.

Suddenly I was aware that two more Hork-Bajir were standing behind me. Not in line to feed. Standing poised. Ready.

I felt the sudden spike of Odret's fear.

"Come with us," one of the Hork-Bajir said.

Odret hesitated. But only for a moment. He knew it was pointless. The Hork-Bajir were Controllers. They were following orders. Nothing he could say would change their minds.

They marched me into one of the shabby, temporary office buildings. It looked like an old barracks or something.

Odret knew who was waiting for him. When the Hork-Bajir opened an office door he was not at all surprised to see Visser Three in his Andalite host body.

<Ah, Odret-One-Seven-Seven,> he said.

"Visser," Odret answered neutrally.

<You've come to feed?>

"Yes. Obviously."

<Then I'm sorry you've been at all delayed. Go. Enjoy.>

Odret did not move a muscle. He knew.

Visser Three laughed. <There is just one thing before you go, Odret. I'll need the truth.>

"What truth is that, Visser?"

The Andalite body moved with liquid ease. The mouthless Andalite face moved to within inches of my own. Both main eyes and one of the stalk eyes bored into me. <I know that you are faithful to Visser One, Odret. That much I know beyond all doubt.>

Odret's fear was seeping into me. Releasing my own adrenaline.

"I serve the Council of Thirteen, Visser Three, as you know. And if any harm should come to me they would investigate very thoroughly."

The visser was unimpressed. <As I said, Odret, I know you are Visser One's minion. The question is about the order you transmitted to me. The order to avoid open war on the humans. I need to know whether that order came from the council, or whether Visser One is its source.>

"I gave you the orders of the council," my mouth said.

<Maybe. And if so, I shall have to obey them.

But if you speak only for Visser One . . . well, that's a very different matter.>

"I've told you —"

The Andalite tail flew so fast that human eyes could not track it. The blade stopped a millimeter from my jugular vein.

<Yes. I know what you say now. The question is, what will you say in a day or so? What will you say when you are starving, Odret?>

I felt the Yeerk's fear rise several more notches to an intolerable level.

"You will pay for any harm that comes to me! You don't dare to defy the council this way!"

<Very simple, Odret: Work for me, and feed. Work for Visser One, and starve. Take him away.>

I saw in Odret's mind's eye the results. So did he. Kandrona starvation was a horror that could not be endured.

I looked straight into Visser Three's Andalite eyes. "The council knows nothing. Visser One hopes to convince them to restrain you. She sent me to delay you till the council issues the order. But it will come."

Visser Three nodded. <As I suspected. I will have to move quickly. Very quickly and present the council with a done deed. Then their order will be irrelevant.>

"I work for you, then?" Odret asked pitifully.

Visser Three laughed. <You betrayed Visser One, Odret. Should I keep you around to betray me? Kill him.>

A Hork-Bajir pressed a Dracon beam against my head. I felt it. Felt Odret's terror. Felt my own shock, fear. Regret.

"No!" my mouth cried. "NO!"

Felt slight pressure as the Hork-Bajir's finger tightened.

Felt —

CHAPTER 23
Jake

DAY FORTY

It was almost impossible following Tom. We tried, but he could drive, and none of us could.

Marco and I searched his room when he was out.

"Careful. Watch for any kind of little telltales he might leave," Marco said.

"What are you talking about?"

"He might place a hair in a certain way, say, wedged into a drawer to see if it's been opened."

I stared at my friend. "What do you know about this?"

He grinned. "I read, man. You know, books? John le Carré. Tradecraft, dude. It's all about tradecraft."

I was going to ignore him. Then I saw the hair.

It was wedged into the closet door so that if the door was opened it would fall.

Marco noticed and gave himself a little, "Am I smart, or what?" flourish.

I took the hair. Opened the closet and searched it carefully. Nothing. I replaced the hair carefully and closed the door.

"Nothing here, man," Marco said. "He's got these telltales around just to see if anyone's been here. He wants to know if he's suspected of anything. But he's not dumb enough to leave his ray gun just lying around."

I led Marco back out into the hallway, down to my room. My dog Homer was asleep on my bed, snoring.

"Maybe we're just crazy," I said.

The phone rang. I jumped about two feet.

"That's good, Jake, very cool. Not at all like a guilty guy."

I waited two rings to see if my folks were home and would pick up. Then I answered the call. It was Rachel.

"Turn on the TV," she said.

"Why?"

"Just turn it on. Channel nine."

I grabbed Marco and went to my parents' room, the nearest TV. Mine was being repaired. I flipped channels till I saw it.

"What's going on?" Marco wondered.

The screen showed a definitely inhuman face. Two main eyes, two stalk eyes. No mouth. But it was speaking anyway.

I scanned quickly. Channel nine, channel five, channel four, all the local channels were carrying the alien. All but channel seven.

<. . . are a parasite species.>

"What the . . ."

It was the alien. The blue deer. Making his second televised appearance. But this time he wasn't on the news set. This was a remote. Probably on tape.

<In their natural form they are similar to your Earth slugs. They enter the body through the ear canal, releasing numbing chemicals to dull the pain. They wrap themselves around the brain, and tie into all neural functions.>

"He's not making any sounds — he doesn't even have a mouth — but I can hear him," Marco said.

The phone on my parents' nightstand rang. I snatched it up. "Yeah, Cassie. I see it."

<Humans who have been affected become Controllers. They will appear to be normal. But they have lost all control of their bodies. These Yeerks —>

"Yeerks?" Marco echoed.

<— have already enslaved three sentient species, the Hork-Bajir, the Taxxons, and the Gedds.>

"Hork Ba-what? This is some kind of goof?" I wondered.

"On all local channels at the same time?" Marco said. "All but channel seven? This is like a tape loop or whatever. The stations aren't cutting in, they aren't, like, putting any scroll or bug or even a logo under the picture."

"What?"

"Man, do you know anything?" Marco said. "All that stuff that's on the screen. You know, they'd put words under this, a title, like 'alien spokesman,' or whatever. No, man, this is bootleg. Someone is cutting this in."

I nodded. "Only channel seven was prepared. They thought this might happen. They were ready."

<I am an Andalite. My people resist the Yeerks throughout the galaxy. But we are not here in sufficient strength. So you humans must fight. You must —>

The screen went blank. I hit the button on the remote. Channel five, blank.

"They cut him off," I said.

"That's what Tom is, Jake. A Yeerk. Or what did he say? A Controller. My mom, too. She's not dead, she's one of them."

I lifted the phone receiver. "You still there, Cassie?"

"Yes."

"What does this all mean?"

"I watched it and . . . every word he said, I was like 'Yeah, yeah, that's it. That's the truth.' Jake?"

"Uh-huh?"

"We call him Ax."

"What? The alien?"

"I know this sounds crazy. But we're supposed to know him. He's supposed to be our friend. We call him Ax. And sometimes he can become human. Crazy."

"Cassie, nothing sounds crazy. Not anymore."

"What do we do?" she asked me.

I looked at Marco. He jerked his chin toward the screen. Two local newspeople were babbling and looking very lost. ". . . don't know how this person, or creature, or prankster managed to . . ."

I flipped to another channel. ". . . some Howard Stern type of prank. Viewers should not be alarmed. We . . ."

Another channel had gone back to *Jenny Jones.*

"I have to pee," Marco said. He went into my folks' bathroom.

"What do we do?" Cassie repeated.

"I don't know, Cassie. But it's not a joke. It's

real. We have to find out who is taking this seriously: cops, FBI, whoever. We have to let them know what we know. About The Sharing. About Chapman and that Mr. Visser and Tobias."

"And Tom?" she asked softly.

"Yeah," I said. "Yeah. Tom, too." I hung up the phone feeling like a hundred-pound weight was suddenly sitting on my shoulders.

A noise. I spun.

Tom. He was standing in the doorway. I didn't have to ask whether he'd heard. He had. The ray gun in his hand told me he'd heard.

"I can kill you, or you can come along peacefully," Tom said calmly. "Your call."

A flash of movement. Marco charging out of the bathroom, rushing Tom like a linebacker.

Tom sidestepped, tripped Marco with a toe, and bashed the back of his head as he fell past. Marco lay sprawled, stunned, on the floor.

"Let's go. You, too, Marco. And don't make me mad, I have a very busy day ahead of me with all this. If you slow me down . . ."

He let the threat hang.

Down the stairs. I couldn't believe it, couldn't imagine it. Couldn't think of what to say to him. He wasn't him. I had no trouble believing that, because there was no way Tom was doing this. No way.

I wasn't even scared because I could not believe any of it. Impossible. Tom? Not even with an alien in his head. No matter what, Tom wasn't going to hurt us.

Marco and I walked down the stairs, through the empty family room, the front door. I opened the door. A car was just screeching to a halt, there to pick Tom up.

The car door opened. A man's voice yelled, "Look out!"

Tom flinched. Too late! The baseball bat came down hard on his gun hand.

"Ahhh!" he yelled.

The ray gun clattered down the steps.

The bat came up fast, caught Tom in the face. Then, one! Two! Three!

Three stiff, hard blows and Tom was down, curled in a ball, groaning, eyes rolling, blood gushing from his nose and ear.

I stared at my cousin. Rachel was breathing hard. But her outfit, hair, and makeup had remained perfect.

CHAPTER 24

Rachel

Tom was down. Someone was running from the car. Someone big.

Jake dove, landed hard, but snatched up the ray gun. He rolled, came up to his knees, and yelled, "Freeze!"

It was so *NYPD Blue.*

The running man slowed, raised a weapon . . .

"Shoot!" Marco yelled.

Tseeeew!

Bright light stabbed from the weapon in Jake's hand. The man screamed. His left leg below the knee no longer existed.

He fell, and fired wildly. The ray sliced into the eaves of Jake's house.

"The car!" I cried.

Jake took aim, fired.

Tseeeew!

A hole burned and sizzled in the car's engine compartment.

Tom was getting up, staggering down the stairs, trying to catch us from behind. I swung low, caught him in one knee. Hard. He went down. He wasn't going to be walking anytime soon.

The injured guy from the car was groaning, rolling onto his side, ready to shoot again. I was on him.

Wham!

People will drop a weapon really fast if you hit their arm with a baseball bat. I grabbed the ray gun.

The driver of the car was out on the street, running, yelling into a cell phone.

"Shoot him!" I yelled at Jake.

"No, he's leaving."

I raised my newfound ray gun and took aim at the fleeing man. Jake yanked my arm upward as I squeezed the trigger. I sliced a couple of branches off an elm tree.

"We don't shoot people in the back," Jake snapped. "And we don't shoot people who are willing to leave us alone."

I shoved his hand away. "Hey, who died and made you president? What are you, the boss?"

"Yes," he said. Then his expression softened. "And by the way, thanks."

"No problem, cousin," I said. "What about Tom? What about that guy there?"

"They'll have reinforcements here soon," Jake said. "We have to get out of here. Cassie. We have to get her before they do. Tom knows I was talking to her."

"Yeah," I agreed, feeling a sudden pang of worry for my best friend. I'd come to Jake's house right away, as soon as the alien was off the air. We live just two blocks apart, less if you know the backyard routes. Cassie lived farther away.

Tom had dragged himself painfully to the steps. He was sitting there holding his knee, not sure which part of him hurt worse.

"You can run, but you can't hide," he said, spitting blood through his teeth. "We'll take you. We'll take you all!"

"Where's that baseball bat?" I wondered.

"The soft invasion is over," Tom jeered. "The real war is about to begin. We'll have you all! You're our meat! You're our *meat*!"

"Come on," Jake said softly. "Quick, before another carload of —"

"Forget carload," Marco said.

He was looking up toward the sky. I followed the direction of his gaze.

It was not a plane. It was not a weather balloon, or swamp gas, or a trick of the light. It looked like a stylized metal cockroach, only where there might have been legs there were just two forward-aimed, serrated spears.

It was, beyond any doubt, an alien ship. And it was slowing as it approached Jake's house.

"Run!" Jake yelled.

"Yes, run! Run! Run, ah-hah-hah-hah," Tom jeered giddily. "Run, humans, run!"

TSEEEEEW! TSEEEEEW!

Two huge beams of light chewed furrows in the lawn on either side of us.

We ran. Across the lawn, the next lawn, the next lawn.

TSEEEEEW! TSEEEEEW!

A garage to our left blew apart, burning splinters.

Marco tripped. I grabbed him and hauled him to his feet. We turned a corner. Jake yelled, "This way!"

We scrambled over a fence, raced through a backyard. I jumped a Big Wheel. Another fence, taller. No problem. Amazing what you can do when you're being fired on by a spaceship hovering a few hundred feet up in the air.

TSEEEEEW! TSEEEEEW!

The pool in the next yard blew up in a geyser of steam. My face stung, eyes watered. We couldn't outrun this thing. There was no way: We were on foot, it flew.

But I had underestimated Jake. He was heading for a little patch of woods over behind the community playground. The trees. He was looking for cover. Just one problem: that was three long blocks and we were already getting tired.

People were coming out of their houses, staring slack-jawed up at the spaceship. The aliens weren't even bothering to hide. Tom had told the truth: This was war.

"Rachel! Here. Stand. Aim!" Jake ordered.

I stopped. We were back against a tin toolshed. The ship would reappear just over our heads as it came around for another shot. We'd see it just as it saw us.

Jake and I held our ray guns straight up. Marco panted, bent over with hands on knees.

"Fire!"

The steel bug slid into view. Our ray guns burned. The ship jerked. It didn't explode or anything, but it jerked visibly, like someone who's been slapped.

The ship hauled away. We ran.

Two blocks before the ship found us again.

TSEEEEEW! TSEEEEEW!

Three cars and a parked RV blew apart. The concussion knocked me down. I felt grass in my face. My ears were ringing like Quasimodo was in the belltower. My skin was singed. My mind wouldn't come together, little fragments of thoughts, little bits of me . . .

I looked around. Jake was just getting up. He was slapping fire off his shirttail. Marco was on his back like he was enjoying a day at the beach.

I climbed up, woozy, fading in and out, but more or less in one piece.

"Marco! Let's go!" I yelled.

I ran to him. Stopped. Looked down. Not comprehending. Not believing.

Jake grabbed me from behind. "Run!"

"But Marco!"

"Run! Just run!" Jake sobbed. "Run!"

CHAPTER 25

Aximili

DAY FORTY-ONE

Videotapes of the Bug fighter were shown on TV. Endlessly. I watched in a portion of a large establishment called a Circuit City. Circuit City was devoted to archaic electronic devices: computers, videodiscs, music players.

Humans in the establishment stared in disbelief. They shook their heads. They discussed among themselves. Some were of the opinion that these invaders were simply misunderstood. Benign, but provoked by some obscure human behavior.

"They're advanced, right? I mean, look at that thing! If they're way beyond us and all, they must believe in peace."

"Yeah? They have a heck of a way of showing

it. Blowing up a man's garage? And how about that RV? You think insurance is going to cover that?"

"Either way, I'm buying that Sony big screen. I don't want to miss any of this!"

"Yes, sir. Can I interest you in our extended warranty program?"

I had heard similar opinions from other humans. They assumed that technological superiority must necessarily be linked to moral superiority. A natural impulse perhaps for an ignorant and primitive species.

Suddenly all the many TV's went blank. The two humans used small handheld devices to change frequencies. But they, too, were nonfunctional.

The entire establishment had grown very quiet. None of the electronic equipment was functioning.

"Power went out," one man said.

"Uh-uh. The lights are still on. It's not the power."

I used my human mouth to explain what should have been obvious. "Electromagnetic pulse," I said. "The Yeerks have simply fired a burst of powerful radiation that has rendered primitive electronic devices inoperative. Ray-dee-ay-shun. It is a complex word. You will discover that any device containing a simple human computer chip will have been overloaded. Chip is a very short word."

The human looked at me in bewilderment. "No TV?"

"No TV," I confirmed.

"Why would they knock out the TV? Is it all the violent shows? Are they sending us a message?"

"Yes, they are sending you a message," I said impatiently. "The message is: We are coming to enslave and destroy you."

I left the establishment. My duty was not clear: I could attempt to assist human efforts to resist the Yeerks. But how? These people were so primitive their vulnerable circuits were unshielded. How could they resist the Yeerks?

Or, I could try at all costs to contact the home world.

The Yeerks would move quickly to increase the pace of infestation now. And my own actions might have caused them to rush.

How many Yeerks would they have in Earth space? It could easily be a hundred thousand. Or twice that number. Their goal would be to secure the planet for additional shipments of Yeerks.

Newly arriving Yeerks would be a mixed blessing for the enemy. The Yeerks suffered from a lack of sufficient host bodies. Andalite intelligence had always estimated that fewer than one in a hundred Yeerks had a host — mostly Hork-Bajir, Taxxon, and Gedd. Gedds were severely limited as were the Taxxons. The Hork-Bajir were excellent host bodies, but Andalite actions had severely reduced the number of surviving Hork-Bajir hosts.

But here, on this planet, were nearly six billion potential hosts. More than enough to supply every living Yeerk with a human host. Humans were physically unimpressive, but they did have excellent hands and very good senses — all the Yeerks needed.

Six billion hosts. A planet stocked with sufficient raw materials for building ships. If the Yeerks took Earth and held it, they would be unstoppable.

If only the Andalite fleet would arrive. It was a perfect opportunity! The Yeerks would rush transports full of Yeerks, as many as they could move. The ratio of unhosted Yeerks would rise in proportion to the number of hosted Yeerks. A fat target. A once-in-a-lifetime opportunity.

If Zero-space had not changed configuration, the fleet could arrive within weeks. If. Zero-space was inherently unpredictable, altering and shifting randomly. A jump that might take a week one day could take a year the next.

By now the high command realized that our task force was missing. But they might not know why. And they would certainly not guess that the Yeerks had located an almost perfect target species for massive infestation.

The larger war could be won. Right here.

Or lost. Right here.

But the fact, the terrible fact was, that the Yeerks would be more vulnerable once they began shipping large numbers of Yeerks to this planet. And that would not happen until human resistance was subdued.

That is an unhappy thought, I told myself. *These are simple, primitive creatures. But I would not want to see them slaughtered to afford us a tactical advantage.*

What was I to do?

Do both. Contact the fleet. Then help the humans, and forget the fact that helping humans now might cause the Yeerks to be more cautious.

Yes. That would be my plan. The policy of a half-trained *aristh*. How would I ever explain myself to my superiors? I could picture incredulous, outraged faces of great war princes staring at me and saying, <*Your* policy, aristh? Your *policy*? And when, exactly, did galactic policy fall into *your* hands?>

I had walked from the Circuit City, down a hill, closer to what humans called a "mall."

I had a clear view of what happened next. Bug fighters began dropping from the clouds. They landed, forming a loose perimeter around the mall parking area. Hork-Bajir jumped out, armed with Dracon weapons.

An interesting move. Yes, the Yeerks would be able to take several hundred humans at once. It made sense.

Several human cars attempted to exit. They were blown apart.

I had a perfect view as well of the black, dangerous shape that swooped confidently down from the blue sky and settled arrogantly atop the mall roof.

A Blade ship. The Blade ship of Visser Three.

CHAPTER 26

Cassie

Marco was gone. He'd never even been a friend of mine. But now he was gone.

Jake couldn't return home. Tom was there, and Jake had to worry now that his own parents were in the camp of the alien enemy.

Rachel, too, was trapped. Where could she go? She had beaten Tom with a baseball bat.

I called my parents and told them I couldn't come home, either. Tom knew me as well.

My parents demanded that I come home immediately. They told me that in all likelihood these aliens were friendly. This was all a wonderful opportunity for the human race.

Maybe they were naive. Or maybe they had been taken, too.

Jake, Rachel, and I had wandered here and there. We had no real plan. What could we do? What could we do, three kids against the momentous events that were unfolding around us?

The TV showed commentators endlessly discussing what it all meant. Some people believed these Yeerks were the hope of humanity. Some believed the Andalite who had hijacked local stations to broadcast his warning. Some thought it was all a monstrous prank.

President Clinton urged everyone to remain calm. He said that just in case, our military forces were being mobilized.

There was a feeling of everything moving in slow motion. A feeling of a world hovering on the brink of something unprecedented. Waiting. Waiting.

The three of us couldn't do much about any of that stuff. All we could do was keep moving and hope to keep living. We'd hidden in stores, in libraries, in the school, here and there. In plain sight during the day, undercover at night.

"I'll grab us some munchies," Rachel said as Jake and I collapsed into the cheap plastic chairs at the mall food court.

Jake looked unspeakably weary. There were dark bags under his eyes. The eyes themselves seemed to have caved in. He was scared. More, he was devastated. Marco was his lifelong friend. Tom was his brother.

"I hope the animals are okay," I said.

Jake didn't answer.

"I mean, my folks will take care of them," I said. "They don't really need me."

I saw Jake's eyes flicker. He was looking past me. I turned around. A group of people were rushing toward the mall exit door, their voices rising excitedly. They were rushing to see something.

"What is it?" I asked.

"Don't know." He stared. He couldn't see anything more than me, but he must have sensed. "Rachel!" he yelled.

I spotted Rachel at the Taco Bell counter. She had caught the tone of Jake's cry. She snatched up the burritos she'd been paying for and came running.

The crowd at the mall door came rushing back now, running away.

Rachel met us as we started to run.

"Rachel. You know this mall. Where can we hide?" Jake demanded.

"Any of the stockrooms. Um, no, too many people there." She looked around frantically. "Furniture department at the department store. Big armoires and stuff. We can get inside."

Scared as I was, I had to admire the girl. She knew the mall.

We started running. Past Express. Past some shoe store.

People were screaming. Ahead, people running out of The Gap.

Then, it stepped into view. It had to be seven feet tall. It had a tail with spikes like a dinosaur's and big, taloned feet to match. There were blades on its arms, legs, head.

It was a monster of destruction. A creature from a nightmare.

And I said, "Hork-Bajir."

No one asked how I knew. The Andalite had used the word on TV. And this, I knew, was a Hork-Bajir. More of the monsters poured from The Gap.

I should morph . . . what? What was I thinking about?

Behind us, Hork-Bajir coming up the aisles of the mall. Not after us. They were rounding everyone up, forming people into little groups and holding them under guard.

"What do we do?" I cried. "We can't fight those things!"

"I'm going to try," Rachel said through gritted teeth. She drew a weapon from her waistband. One of the ray guns she and Jake had taken. She was grinning. She was vibrating with a dangerous energy.

Back out into the mall. Hork-Bajir had cornered a lot of the shoppers. But other people were running around in panic. One had a gun. He fired at a nearby Hork-Bajir. The Hork-Bajir fired back. The man sizzled and disappeared.

Rachel fired. The Hork-Bajir emulated his own victim.

"Up the escalator," Rachel said.

We ran for the escalator. It was still operating. We ran, taking the moving steps two at a time. Then, at the lower landing, a Hork-Bajir appeared.

He leaped! Jake tried to fire, but the monster was on him. Jake and the Hork-Bajir slammed back into Rachel and me. We rolled, bunched and tangled, while the rising steps kept punching me in the back.

Jake had lost his weapon! Rachel had not. But she couldn't get a clear shot. I dug in my heels, braced her, and yelled, "Do it!"

She fired.

Tseeeew!

The Hork-Bajir sizzled.

We were up and climbing the escalator to the next level. Two more Hork-Bajir!

Tseeeew!

Rachel fired. The Hork-Bajir fired. The escalator slammed us into one of the monsters as he was disintegrating. It was like grabbing an electrical power line. I was knocked flat. Rachel fell on top of me. I watched helplessly as her weapon clattered away.

The escalator deposited us in a heap on the landing. Jake jumped up. The remaining Hork-Bajir loomed over him. Jake looked so small. So weak. There was nothing he could do.

The monster was going to take us. Infest us. The Yeerk pool, that dark cavern, that hellish place. I saw it in my mind, but I had never seen it!

"Why?" I asked the creature as he loomed over us.

He did not answer. Instead, his head rolled off his shoulders, hit the escalator, and bounded heavily toward us. The forehead blades caught. It stopped, staring, expression unchanged.

The body fell. But as it collapsed a thin arm and many-fingered hand snatched the ray gun from its lifeless hand.

We reached the top. And there, holding the weapon, was the blue centaur. The Andalite.

He ignored us and started away. But three more Hork-Bajir were on him now.

He whipped his tail. The closest Hork-Bajir fell. But the other two were too close to avoid.

Slash!

The Andalite's flank was deeply cut. The hand holding the weapon hung limp.

Jake lunged. Slid on the polished marble floor, slid beneath the staggering Andalite, tried to grab the weapon.

But he was nearly stomped by flashing Andalite hooves and the huge Tyrannosaurus feet of the Hork-Bajir.

That's when Rachel stepped swiftly behind one of the Hork-Bajir. She was carrying the head. The bladed Hork-Bajir head. She lifted it high and slammed it down, blades out. She buried the Hork-Bajir's head blades in his comrade.

"Aaahhh!"

Jake yanked the weapon from the Andalite, spun, and fired.

Tseeeew!

A Hork-Bajir dropped, sizzling, seeming to fry as it disappeared.

<Thank you,> the Andalite said calmly.

I bent over and threw up.

<Give me the weapon, please,> the alien demanded.

"I don't think so," Jake snapped.

<I am attempting to save your species,> the Andalite said. <And I observe that you have lost two weapons already.>

Fwapp!

His tail snapped like a bullwhip. It hit Jake's

hand and knocked the weapon away. The Andalite snatched it up with his good hand.

<And now, a third. Again, thank you.>

I said, "Ax! Ax . . . Axim. Ax . . ." The word was there, on the tip of my tongue, but I couldn't quite reach it.

The creature's stalk eyes jerked toward me. <Do we know each other?>

"Yes," I said. I wiped the puke from my mouth with the back of my sleeve. "Not here, not this way. I don't know how, but someway, somehow yes, we know each other."

He scanned behind himself with one stalk eye, raised the weapon, and fired over his shoulder. A Hork-Bajir took a glancing blow that disintegrated his right arm and shoulder. The creature toppled over the rail and fell.

"Andalite!" it screamed.

The effect of that one word was electric. The Hork-Bajir below us who had not seen the battle on the second floor immediately forgot about their human captives.

<Are you able to run on those two legs?> the Andalite asked skeptically.

"Dude," Jake said, "we can fly on these two legs."

<You must lead me to the roof of this structure. There is a very slight chance that we can succeed.>

CHAPTER 27

Rachel

"Follow me," I said. I hauled toward the service corridor that would lead to the roof.

All the bad guys were coming upstairs now. Up the stairs, up the escalators, even trying to jump the fifteen feet or so straight up. And failing.

It was insane! No way we'd make it. We were done for. We were dead. Like Marco.

And yet, I was blazing! I was jazzed like nothing I've ever known before. I had gone after a seven-foot-tall alien monster and taken him down! Me!

Narrow stairs ahead, crammed with what Cassie had called Hork-Bajir.

The Andalite aimed and fired. Smart boy. He fired into the mass on the stairs, not the couple who'd already made it to the top. That would slow the ones coming up and make the couple already up here feel cut off.

We raced past them.

"There! That hallway! Right by Sam Goody!"

Tseeeew! Tseeeew!

The glass front of the CD store blew into shards.

Down the hallway, panting, running, sneakers squeaking on tile. Down, past the bathrooms, turn left.

Tseeew! Tseeew!

I felt the heat of it. Hah-hah! Missed me!

Ten feet to the door. I slammed hard against it. Backed off, scrabbled at the doorknob. "It's locked!"

Fwapp!

The Andalite's tail snapped. A gash appeared in the sheet metal of the door. I reared back and kicked it. It popped open.

Inside a metal stairway. Ten steps and a landing. Ten more and another landing. Ten more and we were at the door that led outside onto the roof.

"Ax, or whatever your name is, shoot the stairs!" Jake yelled.

The Andalite hesitated. I don't think he appreciated being told what to do. But Jake was right.

The Andalite leaned slightly forward and fired at the stairs themselves.

Tseeeeeeeeew!

He held the trigger down till the metal twisted and bubbled and burned away. I had to pull back to avoid having my eyebrows scorched off.

When I looked again two flights of stairs were gone.

The Andalite said, <When we exit, we will need to move swiftly and decisively. There is a ship. We are going to take it.>

"Say what?" I blurted.

<Follow me.>

We opened the door and stepped out onto the acres of gravel roof.

And there, fifty yards away, approximately on top of Williams-Sonoma and Eddie Bauer, crouched a black ship that was all sharp edges and mean attitude.

We started running, with the Andalite out front.

There was a ramp leading up into the ship. Fifty yards. And not a Hork-Bajir in sight. Not a guard. Of course not, why bother? What kind of an idiot was going to try and run *toward* that ship?

Our kind of idiot.

The Andalite kicked up the gravel. We raced along behind him. Something was coming down the ramp.

Tseeeew!

Now nothing was coming down the ramp.

Under the shadow of the ship! We hit the ramp. Hork-Bajir above us.

Tseeeew!

More! Aiming at us.

"Yaaahh!" I screamed and lunged.

I felt the wind off the Hork-Bajir arm as it blew past me. I never felt the wrist blade.

I hit the corrugated steel floor. Rolled onto my side. Saw bright lights and moving shapes. The movements grew slower . . . slower . . .

Stop.

CHAPTER 28

Jake

"Rachel!" I cried.

Cassie was screaming. Screaming like she'd never stop.

I grabbed Cassie. Pulled her to me. Dragged her with me. Couldn't look back. Couldn't see what had happened to my beautiful cousin.

Tseeeew!

The Andalite fired again and again. I saw a ray gun on the floor, clasped in a dead hand. I pried it free.

I was holding Cassie by the hand. Pulling her along with me.

Tseeeew!

I felt the charge jolt my fingers. I let go of a hand that was no longer there.

Cassie sizzled and disappeared. Simply evaporated.

I stared at the blank space where she had been. I stared at my hand. I was moaning. A weird sound. Moaning. Like a hurt animal. No sound that any human would make.

<Come!> the Andalite snapped.

I realized everything was quiet now. The Hork-Bajir bodies were everywhere. The air reeked of charred flesh.

I followed the Andalite, stumbling blindly. Down dim corridors. Past locked steel hatches.

A hatch opened, a Hork-Bajir head appeared. It stared in shock. "Andalite!"

Fwapp!

The Andalite struck. I realized now that it had been hurt again. It was staggering. Bleeding. But determined.

<The bridge. Have to reach the bridge.>

We emerged from the hallway into a wider, more open space. There were display monitors that seemed to hang, formless, in midair. Three monstrously huge centipedes manned controls.

And standing in the middle of it all was another Andalite. Older-looking. Different.

The Andalite called Ax stopped suddenly. He was weaving like a drunk.

<Visser Three,> he said.

<Yes. And you must be the Andalite who es-

caped from the wreck of the Dome ship. How enterprising of you.>

"He's one of your people," I muttered.

<No,> the Andalite said. He sounded weary. <Looks can be deceiving.>

The Andalite raised his weapon.

Fwapp!

The creature called Visser Three struck with his tail. The Andalite stared stupidly down with his main eyes at the stump of his arm.

The Andalite was between me and Visser Three.

I raised my own weapon . . .

Visser Three lunged.

. . . fired.

Tseeew!

Missed!

Fwapp!

I hit the ground.

Then Cassie fired.

Tseeeew!

Cassie?

Visser Three's upper body sizzled and disappeared. The deerlike lower half fell over, lifeless.

"No, no, no!" It was a voice that dripped sarcasm and contempt. But it was annoyed, too. *"She's dead! The girl was dead! This is really too much!"*

Cassie came rushing over to me. She knelt down and helped me to my feet.

The Andalite stared weirdly at me. And more so at Cassie.

"It's breaking up," Cassie said.

"What is?"

She shook her head. "I don't know. I . . . I don't know what to call it. But it's falling apart."

The Andalite calmly shot the three big centipedes. Then he stepped to the controls and seconds later the bridge was sealed off.

<They can break through, eventually. But Yeerks are rigidly structured. All commands must come from the bridge. They will not have an auxiliary control.>

I hugged Cassie close, disbelieving. I'd seen her die. Hadn't I?

"What are we doing?" I asked the Andalite.

<I am currently broadcasting a request for help to any and all Andalite fleet elements.>

"Your guys can save us?"

<No,> he said. <But they may be able to save your people. What we can do is make the arrival of the Andalite fleet less dangerous for them and more beneficial for your kind.>

"How are we going to do that?"

The Andalite didn't answer. Instead he ordered a transparent panel to appear. I was looking out at Earth. I could see the North American continent clearly.

We had lifted off and flown into orbit without my noticing a thing.

And then there was a gorilla. It was just there. Squatting in the corner.

"Oh, this is wrong!" the angry, grating voice from nowhere cried again. *"This isn't it at all!"*

"What's that voice?" I asked. "And what's a gorilla doing here?"

<Gorilla? I'm a gorilla? Ahh! I'm a gorilla.>

Marco? It was his voice. Coming directly from the gorilla.

"It's coming apart quickly now," Cassie said, still staring weirdly around, like nothing she was seeing was real.

"Ax! What is all this? You're the alien, man, what is going on?"

The Andalite winced a little at the question. Then, obviously reluctant to admit ignorance, he said, <I do not know.> He looked at Cassie with both stalk eyes. <Perhaps *she* does.>

"It's all a part of it," Cassie said in a sort of whisper. "It's coming apart."

<There it is. The Yeerk pool ship,> the Andalite announced.

"What now?" I demanded.

<Now, I will aim every weapon this ship possesses — and it possesses a great many very

powerful weapons — and I will annihilate the Pool ship and every Yeerk on it.>

<In five seconds . . . >

<Four . . . >

<Three . . . >

CHAPTER 29

Jake

<Two . . .>

"Oh, all right, all right!" the disembodied voice cried. *"Stop it, stop it."*

A thing, an alien, I suppose, something, anyway, that looked an awful lot like a small dinosaur with the skin of a prune, appeared.

The Andalite stepped back from the controls, ready to shoot this latest enemy.

He fired. The energy beam traveled half the distance to the alien, then froze. Simply stopped.

"It was the girl, wasn't it?" the prune thing said, rolling its green-rimmed eyes upward. "She corrupted the time flow."

Now a second figure appeared. He *could* have been a little old man. If you ignored the fact that he was kind of bluish. And glowing. I had the sense that he was no such thing, but that was his appearance.

This creature, this old man, laughed. "It's not so easy, is it, Drode?"

"You cheated me, Ellimist," the Drode snapped. "We had a deal, a trade-off. You were allowed to meddle with the time line in the *Falla Kadrat* situation, and we, my master Crayak and I, were to be allowed to tempt this young jackal here." He stabbed a finger at me.

"I kept my bargain," the Ellimist said. "I have done nothing to bring about this result. The girl is an anomaly. She is sub-temporally grounded. You were careless."

"She's a freak of nature!" the Drode screamed.

The Ellimist nodded. "Yes. She is."

Marco said, "What is going on here?" He was no longer a gorilla. "I'm pretty sure I was dead, then I'm a gorilla."

"Oh, I see it now, I see it now," the Drode said, ignoring Marco, ignoring all of us. "Subtle as always, Ellimist. Your meddling came *before*, didn't it? How could we not have seen it? Elfangor's brother? His time-shifted son? This anomalous girl here? And the son of Visser One's host body? A group of six supposedly random humans that contains those four! You stacked the deck!"

"Did I?" The Ellimist laughed. "That would have been very clever of me."

The Drode spat in disgust. "You knew the girl was an anomaly. You knew she was sub-temporally grounded. And you knew that whatever time line I built, her presence would eventually destabilize it. She knew from the start that the time line had shifted. She felt it. I might as well have terminated this exercise then. I saw the sudden, inexplicable transportation of the mother, I thought, well, it's a glitch! The hands morphing to tiger. All the little breakdowns of logic and sequence. I still thought it might hold together."

Cassie said, "Is anyone going to tell us what is going on here?"

The Ellimist winked at her. And suddenly, alive, in the room with us, were Rachel and that kid Tobias.

"Does this feel more right, Cassie?" the Ellimist asked.

She nodded. "This is everyone. Only Tobias should be . . ."

As I watched in amazement, Tobias seemed to melt, to shift, to dwindle. In seconds there was a hawk where he had been.

"Most creatures live entirely within their time line," the Ellimist said. "Like a person trapped in a single room. They see only what is within those four walls. Others . . . like yourself, Cassie, can see beyond those walls. Can see other rooms, as though the walls were translucent. You felt the change. You sensed that things were not right. You could see, only dimly, but still you could see beyond. You could see what *should* be, where you belonged, and without consciously knowing it you were working to repair what had been torn apart. To reconstitute time as it should have been. You were a virus in the software. You degraded the subtle workings of the Drode's artificial time shunt."

"I have absolutely no idea what you're talking about," Cassie said.

"You were *in* this time line, but *of* another. That is an anomaly. An impossibility. One of the two time lines was doomed to fail. You grounded the true time line. And thus, this time line began to fall to pieces."

"Who are you two?" I demanded of the Ellimist and the Drode.

"He's an old cheat," the Drode snapped. "There are rules, Ellimist!"

"Yes. And I obeyed them. I allowed you to create this alternate time line. And in this time line these humans and this Andalite came very close to annihilating the Yeerk presence. *You* suspended the exercise. Not me. You can continue this time line, or allow these young ones to return to their own times."

The Drode's face was twisted with hatred. "Crayak will have *him* yet."

He was talking about me. I knew it suddenly. I knew who I was. I knew it all. I was myself once more. Leader of the Animorphs.

With that knowledge came a sledgehammer of guilt.

It was all my fault! I had weakened. I'd said yes to the Drode. I'd given in. Marco, Rachel, Cassie, Tobias, all dead — at least in this reality — because I had weakened and taken the Drode's offer.

"Perhaps, Drode. Perhaps Crayak *will* have him," the Ellimist said. "But, then again, perhaps he will have Crayak."

The Drode disappeared. The six of us, the Animorphs, stood there on the wrecked bridge of the Blade ship with the nearly all-powerful creature called the Ellimist.

"At least we'd have won in this time line," I said.

He shook his head. "Yes. But you all would have died. And millions of humans, too, before the victory."

"I gave in," I whispered. "I gave in."

"You have been strong for a long time," he said.

"He shouldn't have to be," Rachel erupted angrily. "None of us should have to. This is enough. This has gone on too long!"

Tobias said, <I *wouldn't*. I wouldn't have done it, would I? I couldn't have ever gone to The Sharing. That was wrong. No way.>

"Of course you wouldn't," Rachel growled.

I said, "Ellimist, is there anything better in our real time line? Will it happen any better, there? Will it, at least, ever end?"

The Ellimist looked at me. Just at me. Sadly, I thought. Pitying.

"It will end," he said. "It *will* end."

I wanted to ask him more. But I knew that was all I'd get.

"So, what happens now?" Cassie asked.

The Ellimist took her hand and held it affectionately. "What will happen now? Only you will ever recall so much as a dim memory of this time line."

Cassie nodded, as though she'd half expected him to say that. "But I'll say nothing about it. Tobias can't know that he might have become a voluntary Controller. And Jake can't know that he ever weakened enough to take the Drode's deal."

"You are wise," the Ellimist said.

"Yeah, and I sure don't *want* to know that I ever dated Marco," Rachel added.

"How do we get back?" I asked. "How do we —"

CHAPTER 30

Jake

DAY ZERO

"Help me. I'm cold."

Another battle. Another horror.

Couldn't anything make it end? Was there no way out? Was I trapped, fighting, fighting till one by one my friends died or went nuts?

I lay on my bed. Stared up at the ceiling.

"Help me. Please. I'm cold."

Into the cave, Cassie.

All for what? For nothing. To delay the Yeerks, but never to win. And someday, to lose.

Was there no way out?

"There's always a way out, Jake the Mighty," a voice said. "My lord Crayak holds out his omnipotent hand to you, Jake the Yeerk Killer. Jake the Ellimist's tool."

I sat up. I knew the voice.

The Drode stood by my desk. It wasn't large. It perched forward like one of those small dinosaurs. It had mean, smart eyes in a humanoid head. It was wrinkled, dark green or purple maybe. So dark it was almost black. The mocking mouth was lined with green.

The Drode was Crayak's creature, his emissary, his tool. Crayak was . . . Crayak was evil. A power so vast, so complete that only the Ellimist could keep him in check. A balance of terror: evil and good checking each other, limiting each other, making deals that affected the survival of entire solar systems.

"Go away," I said to the Drode.

"But you called me."

"Go back to Crayak. Leave me alone."

The Drode smiled. He got up and moved closer. Closer till his face was only inches from my own.

"There *is* a way out," the Drode whispered. "Say the word and it never was, Jake. Say the word, Jake, and you never walked through the construction site. Say the word and you know nothing. No weight on your shoulders. Say the word."

"Go away," I said through gritted teeth.

"How long till your cousin Rachel loses her grip? You know the darkness is growing inside her. How long till Tobias dies, a bird, a *bird*! How can he ever be happy? How long till Marco is forced to destroy his own Controller mother? Will he survive that, do you think? How long, Jake, till you kill Tom? Then what dreams will come, Jake the Yeerk Killer?"

"Get out of here. Crawl back under your rock."

"It will happen, Jake. You know that. The cave. The day will come. You know what the cave is, Jake. You know what it means, that dark cave. You know that death is within. When she dies, when Cassie dies, it will be at your word, Jake."

I covered my face with my hands.

"My master Crayak offers you an escape. In his compassion Great Crayak has struck a deal with that meddling nitwit Ellimist. Crayak would free you, Jake. Crayak would free you all. All will be as it would have been if you had simply taken a different path home."

I saw that moment again. At the mall. Deciding whether to take the safe, well-lit, sensible way home. Or the route that would take us through the construction site, and to a meeting that would change everything.

Undo it. Undo it all. No more war. No more pain and fear and guilt?

"Just one word, Jake," the Drode whispered. "No . . . no, *two*, I think, one must not sacrifice good manners. Two words and it never was. Two words and you know nothing, have no power, no responsibility."

"What words?"

"One is Crayak. The other is *please*."

I wanted to say no.

I wanted to say no . . .

I wanted . . .

I opened my mouth to speak.

"Oh, forget it. Never mind," the Drode said angrily.

Don't miss

ANIMORPHS®

#41 The Familiar

DEE-DEET! DE-DEET!

The alarm was like a jackhammer to the head. I groaned.

DE-DEET!

Enough, already! I felt for the clock radio. The snooze button. Just five more minutes.

My hand patted the air vainly. No bedside table? I lifted my lids. Where was my . . .

My heart stopped.

I was staring into a triangular screen. A flat computer panel mounted flush in a peeling, white plaster wall across from the bed. Eerie copper letters pulsed at the top of the glowing gray screen. 5:28:16 A.M. Below the time flashed the words "TO DO" and a single entry: "Report to work."

This was not my room. Not even close.

DE-DEET! DE-DEET!

My body stiffened to warrior mode and I bolted out of bed.

The alarm broke off.

My mind, forced back into consciousness by the shock, hurled me orders. "Get out!" it warned. "Get out, get out, get out!"

I raced to a tall black panel in the wall. A door. Had to be.

Get out!

I tried, but there was no handle. No release lever. Nothing.

I struck it.

"You are not prepared to leave for work!" said a shrill computer voice.

I pounded even harder. Hammered the panel with a clenched fist. A fist that . . .

I stopped suddenly as I studied my fist.

It was big.

I mean it was rough and callused and had veins that pumped across the hairy, muscular forearm like I belonged to Powerhouse Gym and actually used my membership.

It was the arm of a grown man.

My heart started up again, pumping now at record speed.

I probed the polished steel door frame for my reflection, for the face I knew.

And yes, there! I saw my eyes, dark as midnight. My strong, broad face. My . . .

I swallowed hard.

My short-cropped hair? My six-foot frame?

My day-old beard?

I brought a hand to my face. My fingers scraped across my chin. Stubble like sixty-grit sandpaper. I needed a shave.

My breath got choppy. My head felt about ready to explode.

The Jake staring back at me was an adult! Not crazy old. But out of college a few years. At least ten years older than the kid I'd been the night before.

What was going on? Where were the others? How did I get to this place?

I was gonna have a heart attack if I didn't calm down. I stumbled back to bed and sat down on the narrow strip no wider than a torso. A pad on a metal plate.

"Okay," I said out loud. "Okay." Use your brain. Cover the possible explanations.

An Ellimist trick? Yeah, it had to be. But why hadn't he spoken?

A Yeerk experiment, maybe? Could I have been captured?

It's hard to think straight when you wake up like Tom Hanks in that movie *Big*. At least he woke up in his own room, in his own clothes. Sort of. I was wearing this weird, faded orange jumpsuit, the color of a sun-bleached Orioles cap.

I fingered the suit, and then it hit me.

Of course!

I knew what was going on here. It had finally happened.

I knew it was only a matter of time, what with the pressures of leadership, the violent battle, the endless fights against a strengthening enemy.

I'd finally been driven to a complete psychotic breakdown.

And this was my padded cell.